THE ULTIMATE WEAPON

John Rourke was suddenly in the middle of a small war. Vehicles streamed from the entrance of the Underground City, heading toward the huge overturned trailer. Helicopters airborne in the night sky poured fire on the vehicles. A cylinder larger than the kind used for underground gasoline storage before the Night of The War lay half in, half out of the trailer. Men in gleaming silver decontamination suits clambered around it.

Russians fighting Russians, Rourke realized. Whatever was in the cannister was valuable enough for Karamatsov to risk everything in battle.

In the distance he could see the outline of a workhorse helicopter moving toward the trailer, a crane dangling from beneath it.

It had to be Karamatsov—in his ultimate bid for ultimate power . . .

THE SURVIVALIST SERIES
by Jerry Ahern

Available wherever paperbacks are sold, or order direct from the Publisher. Send cover price plus 50¢ per copy for mailing and handling to Zebra Books, Dept. 1972, 475 Park Avenue South, New York, N.Y. 10016. Residents of New York, New Jersey and Pennsylvania must include sales tax. DO NOT SEND CASH.

THE SURVIVALIST

THE TERROR   #14

BY JERRY AHERN

ZEBRA BOOKS
KENSINGTON PUBLISHING CORP.

ZEBRA BOOKS

are published by

Kensington Publishing Corp.
475 Park Avenue South
New York, NY 10016

First printing: January 1987

Printed in the United States of America

To my good friends Milt Sparks and Dave—all the best . . .

Chapter One

Paul Rubenstein had begun the diary on the aircraft before it had gone down in New Mexico the Night of The War. He had entered into it faithfully ever since, until the Great Conflagration (which seemed the best of all the names for the morning when the fire filled the skies and extinguished nearly all life on the planet) and since the Awakening from their sleep in the cryogenic chambers.

He read now, Annie's eyes closed, her head on his stomach, the sound of her breathing even, the bedside lamplight a yellow wash over his left shoulder.

"I married Annie Rourke—Annie Rubenstein. The name sounds odd to me, but soon won't. There was no rabbi. There was no crushing of wine glasses beneath the foot. The man who married us was Lutheran, the religion here. John told me once that people were married in the heart and that words, if they were spoken over vows at all, were no stronger than what was in the heart. As usual, I have found John Rourke to be right as unfailingly he has always been. A week of marriage now and Annie still has not tired of me—perhaps this isn't just a pleasant dream after all. Married as were we was Michael to Madison; Madison and Michael simply pledging vows formally—like Annie and myself, they were married in the heart."

He skimmed over what he had written after that, his eyes stopping. "Sarah is pregnant—Dr. Munchen, who has joined the staff of the German base being constructed here near Mt. Hekla, administered the test. John had already gone, but he knew—more as a man than a doctor himself. With Natalia—she seems very lonely now, and I would say depressed, but there is no time in her for that—and with Captain Hartman and a force of Hartman's men and the aid of the Icelandic police officer, Bjorn Rolvaag (can I ever repay him for saving Annie's life?). John Rourke leads a scouting party into the heart of what was before the Night of The War, the Soviet Union. They search the Ural Mountains in the hopes of finding the entrance to the Soviet Underground City, the base of power which supports Vladimir Karamatsov, Natalia's husband and the tormenter of her soul. More than her love for John, which now seems impossible, it is the very existence of her husband which is destroying her. She somehow blames herself for the evil he attempts to perpetuate in this second-chance world. But when Karamatsov is dead, what will become of her? I have asked myself that question many times. She is one of the finest, most human of people I have ever known. And there is a doomed look in her eyes—John once called them 'incredibly blue'. Now, they are also incredibly sad. They search for the entrance into hell so they can choke off the supply lines to the devil himself.

"I should be with them. Michael has spoken to me of this. That he and I should follow after them. But John told us to remain here, to help with the building of the base, to serve as liaison between the Germans and the Icelandics. I don't know what to do? Elaine Halverson and Akiro Kurinami have returned to the

8

Eden Project Base. Commander Dodd has entered into the alliance with the government of New Germany, but I fear that Dodd cannot be trusted. He seems at once a weak man and a man obsessed with power. This is unfair to say and I have only shared these thoughts with my wife and with no one else. Nothing Dodd has done has shown him other than conscientious and honest, albeit inept at times. But still—

"Elaine confided to Annie before leaving that Akiro asked her to marry him, despite the difference in their ages and their races. And that she told him yes. Annie has made me promise that somehow when Akiro and Elaine are married, I will get her to the wedding. I promised and somehow I'll keep the promise. But it will mean seeing Dodd again and some of the others there at Eden Base and the thought makes me cold because I remember what they tried to do to Natalia, would have done. How they attempted to keep Michael and Madison and myself from going after Annie when that bastard Blackburn kidnapped her.

"Annie told me everything that happened the night she killed Blackburn. I feel a pride I've never known before that she did what she did to save herself for me."

Paul Rubenstein closed the diary and looked at the quiet, the peace of Annie's face.

Neither of them had ever had anyone before and the night of their wedding; somehow, inside him very deeply, he knew that it had never been better for two people. The great religions all spoke of Paradise after death—but here was Paradise in life. He touched his hand to her cheek and the corner of her mouth upraised in a smile. He brushed the hair from her eyes, and she moved closer against him. He set down the diary, switched off the lamp. As he slid down against the headboard, Annie whispered, "Go to sleep," and slid up into the crook between his right arm and his shoulder.

Paul Rubenstein held his wife very tightly in the darkness and could not sleep yet . . .

It was never dark here. It was always warm here. They had made love and neither of them had felt like sleep. Michael had pulled on a pair of jeans and a pair of the leather slippers made here, given him as a wedding present by Doctor Land who seemed, unofficially, to be the closest confidant of Madame Jokli, the President. Madison had whispered to him once that she wondered if Hakon Land and Sigrid Jokli were lovers.

It was the sort of thing a woman wondered more than a man, he had told himself, but realized he had considered the question too. As Michael had dressed, so had Madison—still the baby she carried didn't even show—in nakedness, or in the tight bodiced ankle length dress she wore.

He had changed guns again—the .44 Magnum Smith & Wesson 629s spoke with authority, but lacked the firepower for prolonged, close range battle. He had seen that when his father had almost single handedly used four .45 automatics to battle and win against the considerable Soviet force which had held Madison, Annie, his mother, and Madame Jokli hostage.

What four .45s would do, two 9mms would do according to some ballistic theory, equally as well or better. He had tried Natalia's Walther P-38—and liked it. He had tried the Beretta 92SB-F military pistol Annie had, carried now in addition to her Detonics Scoremaster. The Beretta handled as well as

10

the Walther and had approximately double the firepower. Beretta pistols had been among the survival stores of the Eden Project, buried in the first of the underground caches opened. He had asked Dr. Munchen—and Dr. Munchen had brought them. Two pistols, twelve spare fifteen-round magazines, four twenty-round magazines and several cases of 9mm ammunition. The ammunition was not from the storage cache, but manufactured fresh, identical even to the Federal Cartridge Company headstamps, but by the government of New Germany in Argentina, as a favor provided by Colonel Wolfgang Mann. Natalia had needed it for the P-38 she carried occasionally and Michael had gotten Munchen to expropriate some of the 115-grain jacketted hollowpoints for his— Michael's—use.

Michael had practiced with the pistols, daily—he had become as proficient with them as with his .44 Magnum revolvers, and then surpassed that level. Leather here was used for boots and scabbards and slippers—like the slippers he wore as they walked along the garden paths beneath the purplish light. But the leather makers were excellent craftsmen and with his father's help, before his father had left, Michael had designed double shoulder holsters, like those his father wore, but with the addition of a thumb break to the trigger guard break. Just as fast. The harness was different as well—but it suited him. He had gotten the leather craftsmen to copy the Milt Sparks Six-Pack his father used for Detonics magazines, but as a four pack instead. As Madison and he had dressed, he had begun automatically to don the double shoulder holster with the Beretta pistols, but Madison said to him, "Do you need to?"

He had smiled, taken her into his arms, left the pistols, instead taking the four-inch 629 and stuffing

it into the waistband of his Levis under his shirt—
armed without appearing armed.

They had begun their walk.

The idea of marriage had a little frightened him,
but when he thought of Madison, the fright quickly
faded into happiness. She was gentle, loving, all that a
woman should be, a quick intellect under the natural
shyness, courage but of the reluctant kind. They
would have a fine child—if a girl, Michael hoped she
had her mother's beauty, the beauty soft, yet classic,
subdued yet penetrating.

He held her hand.

They walked.

Her quiet voice. "I'm happy here, Michael. These
people—they are so—well—"

"I know. When I do go to join my father, well—you
stay here with Annie and Mom. You'll be safe here
with that German base sitting right outside our door-
step."

"I don't want you to go, but I know you have to."
And she hugged her arms around his arm, still
keeping her hand locked inside his. She leaned her
head on his right shoulder. "I was so happy for your
mother, Michael—a baby. Like ours," and she leaned
up and touched her lips to his cheek.

"I love you," he whispered to her.

There was movement from the peach orchard on the
left of the garden path. Michael's eyes flickering
toward it, his right hand freeing itself of Madison's
left hand, of the web of her arms about his right arm,
his right hand grasping past the tails of his shirt, for
the butt of the four-inch 629. The movement from the
orchard had substance now. Three Soviet soldiers in
camouflage fatigues, silenced automatics in their
hands, looks of grim determination in their eyes
beneath the peaks of their caps. He had the revolver

in his fist, shoving Madison back, shouting to her, "Run, Madison!"

He couldn't tell from sound, or from muzzle flash, because there seemed to be neither, just a clicking sound of a slide moving out of battery and back into battery. Michael dodged right to shield Madison with his body as he fired almost point blank into the chest of the man who had just fired. The roar of the gunshot echoed and re-echoed in the night.

There was a scream.

Michael's body turned cold and chills tracked along the length of his spine . . .

Paul Rubenstein opened his eyes. Annie was stirring beside him. He heard a second shot.

"Holy shit," he hissed, rolling naked out of the bed, his left hand groping in the darkness on the floor beside the bed for the Schmiesser, his right hand for the robe on the chest at the foot of the bed as he was to his feet, already running. "Annie! Stay here!"

"No—I'm coming with you!"

"Get a gun!"

Paul was through the doorway, realizing his semi-nakedness now, the robe only half on, not closed, the corridor of the dormitory-like structure flooding suddenly with humanity. A woman in a nightgown with a shawl wrapped about her screamed and drew back as he ran past, saying to her, "Excuse me," and wrestling with the robe to close it over him with his left hand, the German MP-40 submachinegun in his right hand. He shouted back along the corridor, not looking. "Annie—bring me some extra magazines!"

Running—the boom of another shot. Paul Rubenstein shouldered past one of the Icelandic policemen, taking the steps down from the dormitory two at a time, nearly losing his balance, jumping the last four steps, just realizing then that he was barefoot.

Running—a fourth shot. The caliber was unmistakable—it was one of Michael's .44 Magnums.

Clicking sounds to his right, in the direction the shots had come from, along the boundary of the main mall. Paul Rubenstein cut hard right, his feet screaming at him as the naked soles impacted the woodchips there beneath the trees. A uniform—camouflage—a man with a pistol with a longish silencer at the muzzle.

Rubenstein swung the Schmiesser toward the man, working back the Schmiesser's bolt. "Hey—Ivan!"

The cammie-clad man with the silenced pistol wheeled, Paul Rubenstein triggering a three-shot burst, then another three-shot burst, the man's body jackknifing as it tumbled backward. Paul paused for an instant beside the body, kicking the pistol away in case the man wasn't quite dead—he stubbed his toe on the pistol.

The booming of Michael's revolver again—a fifth shot.

"Shit," Paul snarled, breaking from the tree cover into one of the garden paths.

Michael Rourke, Madison's long blond hair and long pale blue skirt visible beneath him.

Michael had the revolver in his right fist, his face a mask of agony, dead Soviet soldiers all around him.

Paul Rubenstein slowed, calling out, "Michael—it's me—be cool!"

He slowed still more, the Schmiesser going out ahead of him like a wand, searching right and left, forward and behind him. He could see Annie coming, running, her long nightgown hitched up to her knees, a shawl half fallen from her shoulders, her hair flying out behind her, a pistol in her right hand.

14

"Take it easy, Annie—I'm not sure the area's clear!" Paul crossed the path, past Michael and Madison, a gathering pool of red blood beneath their bodies.

"Paul!"

It was Annie, and Paul wheeled toward her. She stood on the edge of the path, the hem of her nightgown dropping from her left hand, the shawl dropping from her shoulders, her right arm holding the Scoremaster going limp at her side. She was just staring.

A half-dozen of the Icelandic police came into the pathway, their swords drawn, two of the men shirtless. He shook his head at the swords—he gestured to the Russians dead there in the path and then into the trees, the policemen breaking off in pairs in three different directions, hunting for more of the Russians.

Paul walked toward Annie, taking the pistol from her right hand, noticing for the first time the musette bag with his spare Schmiesser magazines suspended cross body from her right shoulder to left hip, the shawl clinging to it. As he took the pistol from her limp fingers, she walked toward Michael and Madison, the shawl finally falling clear to the surface of the path.

She dropped to her knees, her fists balled tight, the knuckles of her fists against her partially open mouth.

Michael was crying, the revolver set down, Madison's head in his lap, her abdomen covered with blood, her pretty eyes stared blindly open into Michael's face.

Paul Rubenstein turned away for a moment and he started to weep . . .

Annie Rourke shivered, but she had refused to stay

away.

The German soldiers and the Icelandic police stood at attention surrounding the gravesite cut through the ice and into the permafrost. Madison Rourke's body would be perfectly preserved in ice, forever beautiful.

Annie had gone to the mortuary, had personally dressed this girl whom she realized had been her closest friend, her little sister, an angel amidst the hell of earth. She had dressed Madison in the wedding dress. And this was why Annie shivered—partially why. She too wore her wedding dress.

They had found material, lace, worked together, made identical dresses—high waisted, high necked, sleeves which puffed at the shoulder and were very tight and stopped just below the wrist, past ankle length, the skirts very full. Over her dress, Annie wore her heavy coat and a heavy shawl. And Madison, inside the now closed casket—Annie had placed on Madison's head her bridal veil, the veil turned back, and in her hands a crucifix the old man, Jon the swordmaker, had offered for her, and a bouquet of daisies.

The minister spoke in Icelandic, Madame Jokli, swathed in heavy winter garments, her voice choked sounding, translating. "Ashes to ashes, dust to dust—"

Annie's husband, Paul, closed his arms about her and Annie cried. Tears blurred her vision—but through the tears she could see Michael's face and her brother's face was a mask of pain, remorse and vengeance . . .

It had been too early to tell the sex of the child, and the child, boy or girl, would forever rest in its mother's womb. Michael shook uncontrollably, his mother

16

holding his left hand in both of hers, weeping. They had not broken radio silence to contact Natalia and his father with Captain Hartman, not choosing to risk other lives.

He wore the new double shoulder holsters—he would never take them off but to sleep and bathe, until Karamatsov and his Soviet forces were obliterated from the earth.

His throat was so tight that he could barely breathe.

He pulled his hand from his mother's hands and walked to the open graveside, the coffin containing his wife and child not yet lowered.

One of the Germans played a bugle—a trembling rendition of the Star Spangled Banner. Wind-driven specks of ice blasted at his face.

Michael Rourke dropped to his knees beside the coffin, beside his dead wife and child. "Madison— sweet Jesus!" He screamed the words at the wind and at heaven.

Chapter Two

The Soviet infiltration team had been saboteurs—three bombs had been found and disarmed within the crater of Hekla, a half dozen more about the perimeter of the still-under-construction German base, the cemetery where Madison and their child lay between the site of the base and the cone of Hekla itself. None of the bombs had been nuclear.

A Major Volkmer, the base military commander, had doubled the perimeter security and Madame Jokli had agreed that German guards with firearms should supplement the traditionally armed Icelandic police who patrolled the boundaries of the volcano base with only their swords. Two of her police force had been found dead, shot, then the throats slit.

No helicopter had been found—it had been a suicide mission with no means of escape.

Karamatsov.

Michael Rourke watched the moisture from his arctic gear steaming as he sat in Dr. Munchen's office, Munchen having invited him. Munchen entered finally, smiling, saying in his perfect English, "It was good of you to come, Herr Rourke."

Michael nodded, saying nothing, studying Munchen's eyes with his own.

"I'll come to my point then, hmm? So—you are a

young man. You have just lost your wife and unborn child. You are filled with hatred. I simply thought it might be best if we were to talk."

Michael Rourke shifted slightly in his seat, anticipating the conversation, already disliking it.

"I consider your father and mother, though I have only known them a short time, to be among my friends. And since your father is not here, and I have witnessed the grief experienced by your mother, I felt perhaps we should talk."

"Counseling?" Michael asked, not smiling.

"Call it that if you will. What are your plans?"

Michael Rourke shifted his eyes from the eyes of Doctor Munchen, studying his cold weather gear. "What would you do, Herr Doctor?"

Munchen laughed. "You are your father—but in some ways I think you are not."

Michael looked at him, letting his eyes smile. "You didn't answer me?"

"All right," and Munchen lit a cigarette, offering the case toward Michael first who refused with a shake of his head. "Very well. I would blame the so-called Hero Marshal. I would also anticipate Herr Doctor Rourke's reactions once radio silence can be broken or he otherwise learns of your wife's death. I would think that you are even now planning to precipitate some action which will allow you to get to Karamatsov first."

"Very good," Michael almost whispered. "And very correct. I am working under a few handicaps my father doesn't suffer, however."

"Since our base's construction was begun, you have been taking instruction in flying a helicopter. I understand you seem naturally gifted and are doing well, extremely well. That soon you should be able to fly one of our machines with great skill and relative ease."

"Just the excellence of your country's training, Herr Doctor—that's the only reason I've learned fast. I've been soloing since the day of the funeral."

Munchen was silent for a long moment. Then, "You are planning a personal mission against Karamatsov."

"Right you are. If I can borrow a helicopter for the purpose I will. Otherwise I'll steal one."

"You are admirably frank, sir," Munchen smiled, stubbing out his cigarette, getting up, coming around to the front of his desk, leaning against it. His boots shone above and below the discolorations from the snow. "What sort of mission, Michael?"

"Punitive," Michael smiled.

"You wish to find Marshal Karamatsov and kill him before your father can."

"That's the spirit of the thing, yes," Michael nodded.

"Hmm," and Munchen raised his right hand, the fingers splayed. And as he spoke, he lowered the fingers, ticking off item after item. "You have been studying German—doing well there also I understand. You have been reading all the military manuals in our library."

"I'm afraid I understand only a little—I'm about at the talented six-year-old stage with your language."

"What sort of operation do you plan?"

Michael mentally and physically shrugged. "My father and Natalia and Captain Hartman are looking for the entrance to the Underground City in the Urals. But the last intelligence data I heard through Major Volkmer was that Karamatsov was heading for the Mediterranean—what used to be Egypt. Karamatsov's private plane, a large number of his troops, some heavy equipment. While my father is looking for the

Underground City, I'm going to Egypt. It's not all selfish, although there's nothing wrong with selfishness if the concept is properly understood. If Karamatsov is going there, he must be going there for a reason. The desert is probably as forbidding as it would have ever been. Can't be going there for his health. If we could contact my father, he'd be going there too. We need to know what's the reason. I'm going to find out—and if I can kill Karamatsov in the process, all the better."

"Will Paul Rubenstein be going with you?"

Michael shook his head. "Mom's pretty washed out—and so's Annie. Somebody from the family has to be here for when my father finally contacts us. Anyway, the fewer people go, the fewer people get killed if it goes wrong."

Munchen seemed to be reflecting on this. Michael stood up. "I'm running late for my last lesson, so to speak—unless you plan to pull the plug on it. But like I said, if I have to, I'll steal a helicopter."

Dr. Munchen shook his head. "No—I have discussed what I had, it turns out, correctly assumed your plans to be—discussed these plans with Herr Colonel Mann. He too has fears that Marshal Karamatsov is going to Egypt for more serious purposes than seeing if the Pyramids somehow survived the Great Conflagration. And for that purpose, he applauds your desire to pursue this information, despite your bereavement—" Michael stared. Munchen was more complex a man than Michael had supposed. "It is for this reason that I recommended that Herr Colonel Mann secure the consent of Deiter Bern, that you be shown all possible aid. To that effect," and he raised his voice. "Come in, Captain Hammerschmidt!"

Michael wheeled toward the door leading into the

corridor. It opened. A man, tall, gaunt featured, muscular, his face well-tanned, making the eyes bluer than Michael imagined they really were, entered the room, doffing his peaked cap, a shock of close-cut blond hair showing. Following him into the room was a woman and following her six other men, one of them a sergeant, big, burly, a seamed face that was set in a half smile. The woman was tall, nearly six-foot it seemed, thin. But despite the height, she wore medium heeled shoes and her posture was erect, not an attempt to disguise above average female height by slouching—he had seen that in films with his father's videotape machines, read of this anomaly in books—that tall women somehow considered themselves at a disadvantage and, consciously or unconsciously, tried to reduce the appearance of height. This woman did not. Brown hair, the color not spectacular or memorable, simply brown. He couldn't see her eyes clearly—she wore glasses, round-framed, dark-rimmed. The hair hung loosely, almost disorganized but neatly combed. It was past shoulder length. The clothes she wore only seemed to accentuate the appearance of height and thinness—a long, straight skirt that came nearly but not quite to her ankles, the material heavy, like wool, a brown tweed. She wore a sweater, long sleeved, the length almost that of a short skirt, the sweater overly large for her, drooping down at her left shoulder, the sweater gray, a gray blouse visible beneath it, the collar of the blouse tied into a loose bow at her throat.

"Herr Rourke, may I present Captain Otto Hammerschmidt."

Michael Rourke took a step forward, as did Hammerschmidt and they exchanged glances first, then handclasps, Michael finding the grip firm, solid—it went with his first impression of the man.

"Herr Rourke, may I further present Fraulein Doctor Maria Leuden, our greatest living expert on Egyptian culture as it existed since its earliest beginnings until the Night of The War."

Michael looked at the woman—her left hand moved to her glasses, brushed back a strand of the straight brown hair—there was a touch of red in it in the light beneath the overhead fixture. And the eyes were the closest in color he had seen to his mother's eyes, gray-green, what some called hazel. "Fraulein Doctor," Michael nodded, taking her offered hand—there was strength here too.

"Herr Rourke," she smiled, the smile guarded, the voice alto. "I'm afraid the good Herr Doctor," and she nodded toward Munchen, "exaggerates my abilities."

Michael released her hand and looked at Munchen. "I am a great admirer of American popular music from the latter half of the twentieth century. There is a song," and Munchen looked down at his boots, then, his face lighting, he smiled. "Something like, 'I get by with a little help from mein friends—my friends'," and he gestured toward Hammerschmidt, the six soldiers with Hammerschmidt and Fraulein Doctor Leuden. "Your new friends then, Michael!"

Hammerschmidt spoke, "If I may, Herr Doctor, Herr Rourke—" Munchen nodded, Michael watching Hammerschmidt. "It is the opinion of Colonel Mann that Marshal Karamatsov has some sort of hidden weapon. The Herr Colonel discussed this matter with your father," and Hammerschmidt nodded toward Michael. "Colonel Mann further believes that Marshal Karamatsov's expedition to the Egyptian desert is in some way related to this hidden weapon. There would seemingly be no other purpose to it."

Michael Rourke studied Hammerschmidt's eyes, then looked to Doctor Munchen. "And what about my purpose?"

Doctor Munchen's eyes no longer smiled. "If the killing of Marshal Karamatsov can be accomplished, I should think so much the better? Hmm?"

The girl sat down in the chair Michael had vacated, crossing her legs, taking a pack of the non-carcinogenic cigarettes the Germans had from the right pocket of her skirt, a silver cigarette lighter from the left, lighting it, exhaling a thin stream of gray smoke through her mouth and nostrils, but saying nothing.

Michael closed his eyes, nodded his head. "All right—we'll do it."

His eyes still closed, he heard Munchen's voice. "Bravo!"

Chapter Three

Michael Rourke stood alone beside the bed. It was cold, forbidding to him now. He didn't think of Madison every waking moment, because he planned his revenge for her death, the death of their unborn child. But he realized something—that soon, if he survived, his vengeance would be sated by the blood of Vladmir Karamatsov.

And then there would be nothing left but to remember.

The loss of all the children he had played with, gone to school with before the Night of The War. It had never been personal to him—there had not been time to think of it. He remembered the Jenkins family—the murder of the father, the suicide of the mother unable to cope with the horror, leaving her own child an orphan, his own mother taking the Jenkins girl and finding her a home while they had continued their search for John Rourke.

Death to Michael Rourke had become an impersonal thing inflicted upon the enemy, and there was no shortage of enemy. He had killed his first man before he was ten, stabbing the man in the kidney with a boning knife to save his mother from what he realized now would have been forced oral sex and then rape. He had killed during the defense of the Mulliner farm house.

Killing, but never experiencing death.

He sat on the edge of the bed.

Gentleness—that was Madison. And gentleness in this world was more doomed to extinction than mankind could ever be, Michael Rourke thought.

On the top of the dresser were his weapons.

The dresser drawers were empty, his own clothes that he would take packed, Madison's clothes given to Annie and to his mother. He had kept nothing of her except her memory—he had no picture of her. And her wedding ring that she had given him, hers buried with her and their unborn child. He studied the ring on his finger. It was of stainless steel, high in nickel content, one of two, made for them by old Jon the swordmaker.

Michael turned the ring on his finger—he felt the tightness starting in his throat and chest again and he stood up, shaking his head to clear it.

Old Jon the swordmaker had given another present to Michael the day of Madison's funeral.

The former scientist, his ancestors for generations workers of steel, had crafted for Michael a knife. Michael withdrew the knife from its pouched sheath now, the pouch fitted with a whetstone, one side fine grit, the other side coarse. He turned the knife in his hands, the bowie patterned blade nine inches long, two inches wide, a quarter-inch thick, the handle tubular shaped, six-inches long, more than half its length hollow. The blade gleamed only dully, sandblasted. "I have made a knife for you, Michael Rourke," old Jon had said out there in the snow, withdrawing the plus fifteen inches of steel from the rags in which it had been wrapped. "Before what you and your family call the Night of The War, there were things called knife shows, if I have the term correctly.

My ancestor at that time would visit each of these shows that he could in his travels. When he would see a blade that seemed somehow out of the ordinary, he would ask its maker the permission to take a photograph. It was that way with this blade." And old Jon had taken from the pocket of his heavy overgarment a piece of paper. He read from it. "It was in a place called Texas and he met a man named Crain. In this case, my ancestor," and his blue eyes looked toward Michael's through the swirling snow, "became friends with the maker and eventually purchased one of the knives." And Jon consulted his paper again, a lock of white hair falling across his forehead. "It was called," he read, "a Life Support System I." He looked up from the paper. "After the Night of the War, when things were settled here, when my ancestors could again resume their craft, the knife was copied. There seemed to be no way to improve upon it and the design has been passed down. The blade is hand ground from bar stock—440 C stainless. The hollow handle is machined from a solid block of steel. The guard is double quillon style, three and one-quarter inches long, a quarter-inch thick with holes drilled into each side of the guard for lashing the knife to a pole for use as a spear. The original Crain knife, I understand, had the handle wrapped with nylon cord—this is not available here. Perhaps your German friends would have this. The sheath is made to fit the knife, out of ten ounce leather, and vat dyed so the black color will remain fast whatever you do. You will need such a knife if I read the look in your eyes correctly."

Michael Rourke had embraced the man, words of thanks failing him. The spine of the blade was sawtoothed for emergency cutting of rope, wood or wire. He had secured two hundred pound test braided line from the Germans, let Jon show him the technique for binding it over the handle so both ends of the line would be properly secured without a knot. He had filled the three and seven-eighths inches of storage space with water and wind proof matches, water purification tablets, monafilament line for emergency use (it had once been called fishing line), a magnesium stick for aid in fire starting and other incidentals that might prove of survival utility. There was room in the pouch which carried the stone for a split ring ended wire saw, of the type once called commando saws and useful for sawing limbs or as a garrote. His father had long ago taught him the principles of knife fighting, and as with his martial arts, he practised the katas daily when conditions allowed.

His knife, his pistols, his M-16, his other gear. Michael Rourke looked at his wristwatch, like his father's a Rolex, but a Sea-Dweller rather than a Submariner, black faced, luminous, simply waterproof to greater depths. As a child, he had swum well—he supposed the skill would return if needed.

Once more he stared at the bed.

It was time to go. Paul, Annie, his mother would be waiting to bid him good-bye.

Michael Rourke slipped on the double shoulder holster with the Beretta 92-F military pistols. He unthreaded the belt of his Levis, threading onto it the sheath for the Life Support System I knife, the Milt Sparks-like four pack for the Beretta's magazines, the magazines in place. He picked up the knife, staring at it once more. He sheathed it, secured the safety strap, tied the lace which gave it added security in the leather.

He caught up his pack and the rest of his gear, including the arctic gear. He would need it not at all now—he wouldn't be out in the cold now except for a moment.

Michael looked once more to the bed he had shared with Madison, then left the room . . .

Paul had taken his gear to put it aboard the helicopter, Hammerschmidt at the controls; the woman, Hammerschmidt's sergeant and the five enlisted men already aboard. Michael stood, his arms folded about his sister Annie. "I love you, even if you are my sister—ya know that?"

"Uh-huh—I wish you weren't—"

"I've gotta, Annie."

He felt her nod as she stepped back, still holding his hands. She was pretty—she was always pretty though he had never told her that. Her long hair, darker than the honey blond color of her childhood, the shawl draped about her shoulders, the high necked, laced ruffled white blouse and ankle length dark blue skirt, clothes that were the fashion here. "You take care of Paul and take care of Mom—okay?"

Annie licked her lips, nodded only.

He looked at his mother. Like Annie, the long skirt, the blouse plainer, no shawl, her hair shorter than Annie's hair, pretty—she seemed ageless, looking almost like a sister to him, to Annie, in biological age Sarah Rourke not even old enough to be his mother but for the tricks his father had played with the cryogenic chambers, allowing Michael and his sister to age to adulthood, making parents and children contemporaries.

Michael opened his arms, his mother rushing into them, crying as he hugged her against him.

"I did this all the time—all the time with your father—and now you," and her voice choked off.

"I've gotta, Momma."

She said nothing, just closing her arms about him, holding him. "Be careful." She leaned up to him, smiled, tears filling her eyes, kissing him on the mouth, then nodding her head, the smile broadening. The tears welled from her gray-green eyes and streaming down her cheeks. "I love you."

"I love you too," Michael whispered.

He kissed her cheek, Annie beside him too now, his arms enfolding them both. He whispered, "I love you both," and then started toward the helicopter, its rotor blades turning lazily, Paul standing at the doorway. Like Michael, Paul had not adopted the fashion here—no loose fitting trousers, baggy-sleeved shirt, high boots. Paul dressed as he always seemed to—a light blue workshirt like Michael's father habitually wore, faded Levis, combat boots.

Paul Rubenstein ran his left hand along his high forehead and back, into his thinning black hair, the hand stopping. Paul smiled, looking down suddenly at his boots, his voice lower than it was usually. "Gonna miss ya, Michael."

"Take care of Mom too, huh?"

"They're as safe as a synagogue," Paul laughed. "Church to you."

"Right. I know why you're Dad's best friend—I think you're mine too."

"Gonna get me cryin' too in a minute," Paul Rubenstein grinned, stabbing both hands into his pockets. Since Madison's death, he had not see Paul unarmed—the battered Browning High Power was in the tanker style chest holster—just in case the Russians successfully infiltrated again, Michael knew.

Michael stepped toward Paul, and the two men embraced like the brothers they were, Michael suddenly understood.

"God bless you," Paul whispered.

Michael nodded, both men stepping back, Michael seeing the awkwardness in Paul's eyes that he too had felt at the display of emotion. It was the curse of friendship between men, that somehow there was always appearance to preserve—he suddenly couldn't remember the last time he had hugged his father.

Michael and Paul simultaneously extended their right hands, clasping them. "Be seein' ya," Paul almost whispered.

"Be seein' ya," Michael echoed softly, releasing Paul's hand. He didn't look back as he clambered aboard the German helicopter, but as it went airborne, he did, seeing the three of them, his family, letting the tears come into his eyes because he could no longer hold them back . . .

Snow and ice needles swirled tornado-like, it seemed to him as he jumped from the machine, skidding a little on his combat boot heels. Getting his balance, he hunched his shoulders under his leather jacket, his neck against the upturned collar, his bare hands thrust into the slash pockets of the jacket. He had had the coat made for him here at Hekla. And Hekla loomed intermittently in the distance as for an instant the swirling snows would part, curtain-like.

Michael Rourke stopped walking, standing, then dropped to his knees in the snow—the marker was nearly covered in white. Soon, the accumulating, never melting snow and ice would obscure it completely. He stared at the snow beside the marker and he whispered her name. "Madison."

Chapter Four

John Rourke, Natalia Anastasia Tiemerovna and
Captain Hartman flanking him, crouched low in the
shelter of the high, snow-splotched rocks, the rock,
like the air around them, cold. Pines towered behind
their position, the pine boughs sagging, heavy laden
with snow, the snow brilliantly white against the dark,
gleaming green of the trees.

The sky was gray, overcast heavily and darkly
threatening. Rourke, Natalia and Hartman sought
shelter in the rocks almost as much from the stiff, chill
wind which blew down through the mountain valley
from the north as from the eyes of the Soviet soldiers
who had marched into the valley, entering from the
same direction.

The others of the German force were nearly a mile
away, along the course of what had been a river bed
which now rocky, gravel strewn, cut a jagged scar
along the valley floor to the south.

Spotting the Soviet patrol had at once been comforting and unnerving—comforting in that it confirmed to John Rourke that the Soviet Underground
City was indeed most likely north of them, the
direction in which Rourke and the others had been
searching for the last several weeks. But it was unnerving now—there were more than three dozen of the

Soviet soldiers and at approximate platoon strength it seemed more than a patrol.

The likelihood of detection of the presence of himself and the others in the area was remote. They had moved cautiously, covered their tracks as best they could. But the likelihood still existed.

It was the size of the patrol that was critical because he did not know the usual Soviet patrol strength.

"What do we do, John?" Natalia asked, her voice low, but not a whisper, her blue eyes barely visible above the scarf which swathed her face against the cold.

Rourke rubbed his hands together for warmth, then stuffed them into his gloves. He looked at Hartman, then back at Natalia. He was pleased that Hartman and the soldiers of New Germany were standing up so well to the cold—their home in Argentina never approached the rigors of this climate in the heart of Russia's Ural Mountains.

John Rourke had made a decision—not one that he liked, but a decision nonetheless that seemed best under the circumstances. "Here's what we'll do," he began, glancing behind him and up, over the rocks, toward the sluggishly moving Soviet column. The Russians looked cold—so was he. Rourke looked to the German officer with whom he and Natalia had shared the last several weeks searching. "Captain—if you agree, I'd recommend that you get back to the main body of your men and take them due west about ten miles or so and get them up into the mountains. Find a good defensible location you won't mind living with for a while, but one that will allow radio reception—"

"We will have to get well back under an overhang or find a cave—their aerial surveillance techniques should be sophisticated enough to detect our watch fire."

"Agreed," Natalia murmured, her voice trembling with cold, sounding muffled from beneath the scarf covering her mouth. Rourke jerked his thumb behind him toward the valley below the rocks and the Russian soldiers. "Natalia and I—we'll follow our friends. Eventually, they're going to turn around and go home or send out a courier or get resupplied in the field—something or another that'll lead us to the Underground City. Once we've tracked them back there or otherwise pinpointed the location, we'll contact you by radio. Keep listening for us until we're able to monitor enough of their communications to pick up their busiest times and their unused frequencies—then we'll make a brief contact at precisely six A.M. common time," and Rourke checked the Rolex Submariner on his left wrist, Hartman doing the same with his watch—Hartman set his watch ahead two minutes, then rolled down his storm sleeve.

"Could not we get a triangulation on them—and locate the Underground City in that manner, Herr Doctor?"

Rourke shook his head, Natalia's muffled alto coming again. "They probably have their transmission tower or towers located a good distance from the Underground City, and then complete the communications link by cable, perhaps by laser—who knows?"

Hartman nodded thoughtfully. "When we notify you, I'll give you a number," Rourke continued. "Let's say I give you a number like fourteen—add a certain number to it and you'll get the time to listen for our detailed transmission. And I'm going to rely on your listening because if you transmit an acknowledgment it'll make the transmission too long maybe—maybe long enough for them to pick it up."

"Probably their aerial reconnaissance will pick up

our communications anyway," Natalia added soberly.

Rourke only nodded. "Take the number fourteen and add it to whatever number I give you. If I say fourteen, then you'd listen for us in the morning at four hundred hours with the beginning of the day clock as a base. If I say thirteen thirty, then you'd listen at zero three thirty hours—like that."

"A good plan, Herr Doctor, but I fear a dangerous one," Hartman nodded, his shoulders hunched against the cold.

"Best I can think of," Rourke smiled.

"I have an extra seven days of rations—let me share them with you," Hartman began. "You may need them."

"Agreed," Rourke told him.

"Keep one day's rations for yourself," Natalia said to him. "Give us three and three—you might get pinned down and have to wait. In this cold, going too long without food—" She let the sentence trail off unfinished, looking down into the valley. "They are crossing, John."

Hartman was sloughing out of his pack, Rourke helping him. Rourke divided the rations equally into two piles, Natalia taking a pile and Rourke turning his back to her, feeling her hands as she opened one of the pouches of the Loco Pack and began securing the food inside. He helped Hartman back into the pack, the German officer securing the waist strap. "We need a deadline in the event something goes awry, Herr Doctor."

"Good point," Rourke nodded thoughtfully. "Fine—let's use the rations we have as the determiner. Natalia and I each have ten days worth. If you don't hear from us within that time, pull the plug on the operation."

"Pull the plug?" Hartman repeated, his pale eyebrows cocking quizzically.

"Abort," Natalia said softly.

"Then use your own judgment on whether or not to come after us or go for extraction depending on your situation."

Hartman nodded slowly. "Yes, Herr Doctor, Fraulein Major—good luck—to you both," and Hartman tugged off his outer glove and the liner, Rourke doing the same, clasping the German's hand. He offered his hand to Natalia—still gloved, she took it.

"Wait until we're clear, then move out," Rourke told Hartman, both men re-gloving.

Rourke picked up the Steyr-Mannlicher SSG—when he had returned to the Retreat before setting out for Communist Europe, he had determined that the long range 7.62mm NATO chambered counter-sniper rifle might prove an asset. He checked the lens caps on the 3x9 variable scope. They were secure.

"Ready, John," Natalia murmured, her M-16 in both tiny fists.

Rourke reslung his M-16 cross body under his left arm, carrying the Steyr in his right fist.

He looked once more at Hartman, the German giving a thumbs up signal.

Natalia was already moving, Rourke following her, keeping low behind the rocks, the crunch of new, hard snow beneath his boots, the Russians already disappearing over the horizon.

His breath steamed, the wind lashing at his face and he pulled the ski toque back into position to protect his skin.

Hartman was right, of course—following the Russians was more than dangerous.

John Rourke clamped the still unlit, thin, dark tobacco cigar in his teeth and kept moving.

Chapter Five

They had landed on the west coast of Great Britain and changed to a radical fixed-wing aircraft. Then again they landed, this time for refueling, in what had been, before the Night of The War, Portugal, near Lisbon, which like all other cities on the surface had ceased to exist during the Great Conflagration. They had crossed the southern tip of Spain into what had been Algeria, then refueled once again to avoid touch-down necessity in the overflight across the Libyan desert and on to Egypt, across the western desert.

As Michael Rourke stared downward through a fuselage window, he heard the now familiar German accented, perfect English of Maria Leuden. "Generations passed here without rainfall—odd to consider, I suppose, but here, beneath us, the land was immune to the Great Conflagration. It was already parched far beyond the effects of mere flames."

"The dead are the only ones immune to death," Michael murmured.

"Is that a quotation? From what?" she asked.

"It could be, and if it is I don't know from what," Michael answered her, for the first time turning to look at her. Her hair was gathered back at the nape of her neck in a scarf that looked to be silk—but he had learned that things often weren't what they appeared.

The scarf was tied into a softly drooping bow.

"I must ask you this," she smiled, her gray-green eyes bright, the glasses she wore catching reflected sunlight off the desert floor beneath the ship. "You seem marvelously well educated, but if I understand correctly, you weren't even ten years old on the Night of The War. You have read a great deal, I assume, but still—" She cut herself off, saying nothing, as though waiting, the sentence not needing to be finished, what she had said already enough to convey proper meaning.

"My sister Annie and I," he began, looking from her for an instant, to the drifts of dune beneath them, the gray yellow of the sand, then turning back to look at her, "Annie's the intellect of the family, I'm afraid. She began reading the encyclopedia as soon as she could read well enough to find the words she didn't understand in the dictionary. I've read it too, but really only skimmed. We didn't have that much else to do, really. Practice the skills needed for staying alive, maintain the Retreat."

"This Retreat—Herr Doctor Munchen spoke of it as well. Has he seen it?"

"He accompanied my father to the Retreat when Dad made the trip back there before leaving for the Urals with Captain Hartman."

"What is this place like?"

Michael shrugged, smiled, looked away from her again, his gaze drifting like the sand beneath their racing shadow.

He began to tell her of his world for nearly two decades, his tomb for five centuries and found himself telling her of the days and nights before he had first seen it, of the desperate flight of his mother, his sister and himself, their search for his father, the eventual reunion, of the horrors he had seen on that last morning. "Natalia was preparing the injections of the cryogenic fluid. I was helping Paul, Annie was helping Momma—" He shook his head, his throat tight with the memory. "My dad was listening to ham radio broadcasts—"

"Ham?"

"An amateur short wave radio operator."

"Ohh," she nodded, Michael watching her eyes.

"Cities were going off—it was—ahh—shit—ahh—anyway. He had closed circuit television that was run off cable and you could watch the sky, the lightning. I guess later, Dad watched as the Soviet troops attacked the mountain, watched them as they died."

"A story I heard about your father—Herr Doctor Munchen recounted having heard it when in conversation with your mother and sister and your sister's husband—"

"Paul Rubenstein—and I bet I know the story," Michael smiled. "Annie—I don't know if most women have the ability, but she does—she kept at it until Dad finally told us what happened at the end." He exhaled a long breath. "There had been this American Army officer—Reed. Dad and Natalia—"

"That is Major Tiemerovna? The Russian woman?"

"Yeah," Michael nodded. "Her uncle was the Soviet commander for North America but despite that a good man. When he realized what the KGB had planned, what the fate of the rest of the earth would be, he arranged things so my Dad and Natalia and a group of Soviet Special Forces personnel whose loyalty he trusted could link up with a group of volunteers from U.S. II—"

"That is the interim government that was formed under the man named Samuel Chambers between the Night of The War and the Great Conflagration—

39

correct?"

"Yes—yes, that's correct. All of them—the American volunteers, the Russians, Natalia, my dad—they attacked the KGB cryogenic project called the Womb. The Russians had their particle beam weapons systems installed there. During the raid, well—the raid was successful, the cryogenic materials stolen, the Soviet base destroyed, the particle beam system disabled, but this American officer named Reed—my dad saw Reed climbing one of the particle beam masts, trying to raise an American flag. Reed died before he could do it. I guess my dad figured it was something that needed doing. He used one of the escape tunnels and a hatchway and got up on top of the mountain where the Retreat is. The KGB commander—a guy pretty much like Karamatsov in a lot of ways, I guess—his name was Rozhdestvenskiy. He was in the last Soviet helicopter. My dad had just raised the American flag. They had a duel, right there on the mountain-top, my dad with those little Detonics .45s of his and Rozhdestvenskiy with a submachinegun or something coming at him in the helicopter. My dad was almost out of ammo, and Rozhdestvenskiy's chopper had fired out its missiles and was closing. Dad got him with his last round and killed Rozhdestvenskiy and the chopper blew up just as the flames closed over the top of the mountain. Dad just made it inside. He treated his wound, took care of the last details of securing the Retreat, then climbed into his cryogenic chamber. But before he gave himself the shot of the cryogenic serum we used, he reset his chamber's timer to awaken him earlier than the rest of us. Anyway," Michael exhaled— "Yeah—he's a brave man, my father."

"Someday, historians will write of him."

"Probably. He's always been larger than life."

"Resentment?"

Michael Rourke looked away from the sand and back toward Maria Leuden. "No—I don't think so. Just stating the obvious."

"He must be a difficult figure to live up to."

She was pushing, Michael thought.

"No—Dad taught Annie and I something—well, a lot of things. Everything, really. Almost. But he taught us to live up to ourselves. Be ourselves. Annie. Me. And that's a pretty good way."

"I like you," she told him.

"Thank you."

"I think I like you a lot," and she took off her glasses, closed her eyes and leaned her head back against the rest.

Michael watched her a moment longer, then returned his eyes to the desert . . .

Lieutenant Milton Schmidt sat in the passenger seat of the SM-4, his eyes shaded by the peak of his cap, but the glare of the bleached desert still bright, heat shimmering from it upward on waves of distorted light. His driver stood with the other drivers, talking, smoking, laughter drifting toward him occasionally.

Schmidt contemplated what it would be like to meet a Rourke. He had been at the Complex when this American doctor had aided in securing liberation from the Leader. He had caught a glimpse of the man who was this Rourke's father. The Herr Doctor had been tall and straight and fit and in the brief glimpse Schmidt had gotten of him, there had been a look to the man's eyes. Despite the name, Schmidt was secretly sure that Herr Doctor John Rourke must somehow be German. And he wondered now at the son of this man. The bizarre similarity in the ages of the Rourke family—both generations—had been explained to him before leaving the Complex, explained to him personally by the Herr Colonel Mann. Somehow, the American doctor and his family had survived the Great Conflagration in cryogenic sleep and Herr Doctor Rourke had used the cryogenic sleep to age his children to adulthood, to share in both the dangers and the adventure of the new world into which they awakened.

Schmidt wondered too about Captain Hammerschmidt. He knew the man to see, to salute, but had never worked with the commando leader before. But he knew the man's record—one of Colonel Mann's most valued officers, one of the officers involved in the attack on the SS headquarters at the Complex. Hammerschmidt, to Milton Schmidt, epitomized the German officer corps.

In the distance now, he could see a shape. The flap at the back of the truck parked just ahead of his SM-4 swung upward, a face appearing there. "Herr Lieutenant—it is the aircraft."

"Keep scanning, Corporal—it is possible their flight has attracted some attention from the Soviets."

"Yes, Herr Lieutenant!"

The flap dropped back down against the strong desert sun.

Milton Schmidt climbed down out of the SM-4 and to the sand.

It was one of the new J-7Vs, a dynamically rearswept wing with the jet driven propellers mounted to the rear of the wing surface, a low radar profile and the ability to fly mere feet over the surface, the terrain following ability radar defensive as well. The J-7V, it was rumored, would replace many of the helicopter gunships now diverted from combat roles and utilized for troop transport. Yet, armed as was this J-7V, the new short take off and landing craft was nearly as useful in a military role as the combat gunships.

It swept in low from the west, already starting to climb, necessary he knew from the literature circulated concerning the J-7V, so the changeover from horizontal to vertical flight mode could be accomplished. Climbing—and then suddenly it seemed to stop, unlike a helicopter, more like—he didn't know what. It was sand colored against the blue of the desert sky—there was a tongue of what looked like flame beneath each engine as the engines rotated into the vertical mode and the aircraft began to descend. Unlike a helicopter, it was almost straight up and down, like a plumb line being dropped.

Lieutenant Milton Schmidt pulled his goggles down from above the peak of his cap, against the storm of sand already rising to surround the aircraft.

Soon the true adventure would begin. It would be worth the wait, he somehow knew.

Chapter Six

The Soviet patrol had stopped—it seemed for the night. Natalia, crouching beside him, seemed bone weary. John Rourke folded his arm about her and she rested her head against his chest. Her breathing felt heavy but regular to him. In the mountains, the air was thinner than at the lower elevations and although their bodies had become more accustomed to the generally thinner atmosphere of Earth since the fires which had nearly consumed it five centuries before, the thinness of air still took its toll.

The sun was setting in the west—the direction in which he hoped Hartman had already moved the remainder of the search force.

Tents were going up—inflatable, it seemed, thickly insulated.

Such tents were available to Rourke and Natalia as well—but could not be used lest they be sighted by the Russians.

"We'll have to sleep together," he whispered to her—and suddenly he heard the sounds of her crying and he set down the SSG in a niche of rock and raised her face in his left hand and stared down at her. "What's the—"

"Nothing, John—nothing—"

"What's the matter?"

"What do you think is wrong?" and her eyes, in the half light, seemed flooded with tears. Their blueness hypnotized him as it always had.

"There's, ahh—nothing—"

"When this is over—I have to go away, John. I don't know what I want to do—but I have to go away."

"I know that. Maybe, ahh—at Hekla, with the Icelandic people—maybe—as a scientist, you could—"

She laughed, sniffing back the tears. "But until then we can warm each other, can't we?"

His lips touched at her tearstreaked cheeks and John Rourke held her close against him for a long while, his eyes focusing in the gathering darkness on the Soviet encampment below them . . .

They had sealed together the mummy-style sleeping bags—the Germans had developed insulated padding to what almost amounted to an art. For a people who for five centuries had inhabited an almost perpetually warm climate, who had been on the surface for a comparatively short time, they had planned ahead—and Rourke admired that. The bags weighed virtually nothing, but lofted well above any sleeping bag he had ever used. They trapped body warmth so well that despite the ambient temperature of the night here in the thin air of the Urals, on a mountain peak surrounded on three sides by nothing but sky, the Soviet encampment below them, it was so warm inside the bags that he had stripped away his sweater and opened his shirt front, Natalia's head was against his bare chest, only her nose exposed enough to breathe.

But he moved her gently aside now, buttoning his shirt while still inside the bag—he almost never wore undershirts, despite the climate. And he had chosen against a thermal insulated undershirt for several

45

layers of protective clothing instead—so far his judgment had proven out and he had been more than
adequately comfortable against the cold.

He ducked his head into the sleeping bag, finding
his sweater which had balled up at the foot of the bag
near his feet—pulled it on, pulling on the ski toque as
well and thrusting his head out of the joined bags, his
bare right hand closed on the butt of the Python.

He found his boots and started into them, the boots
freezing cold at first, but the insulation coupled with
the body warmth he had brought to them already
starting to work as he laced them closed.

He shrugged into the double Alessi rig for the twin
stainless Detonics .45s, the shoulder holsters kept
between the mummy bags and the ground mat, the
guns almost warm to the touch. The coat, the special
insulated pants. Before the coat was zipped, he had
the hood pulled up.

He had heard something in the valley. Inside himself, he knew there would be no more sleep tonight.
But Natalia slept and he would let her sleep until she
had to be awakened. He had wronged her by loving
her, letting her love him—loving her but never touching her as she wanted him to, as he had so long
wanted to but never allowed to himself. He looked at
her form as she stirred inside the bag—she would be
warm. "I love you very much," he whispered.

John Rourke stood, buckling on his gunbelt and
holstering the Metalifed and Mag-na-Ported Python,
closing the flap on the holster, checking that the
Gerber knife was in place on his belt. He had never
removed the little A.G. Russell Sting IA Black
Chrome from inside the waistband of the Levis he
wore beneath the arctic outerwear.

He was moving now, the SSG in his right fist, the
scope covers removed to let the lenses adjust to the

46

temperature.

He had chosen a campsite at the height of a craggy precipice overlooking the valley in which the Soviet patrol had encamped, the campsite protected on one side only against the wind but beneath an overhang which would afford practical protection from inadvertent aerial observation. Using some of the Icelandic fuel blocks, he had built a quick hot fire to warm melted snow—it was not radioactive here—and used the melted snow as boiling water to warm the freeze-dried rations they carried. The rations were less imaginative than the Mountain House foods he had always carried prior to the Night of The War. No beef stroganoff, chicken tetrazini, but tasty and healthy and filled with vitamin and mineral supplements. They had eaten with their bodies partially inside the bags, then burned the packaging materials in the last flames of the fiery fuel blocks, letting the fuel blocks burn out naturally to avoid leaving anything too recognizable where they had been. He had made a mental note to cover the small fire pit in the morning.

John Rourke reached the lip of rock overlooking the valley, lowering his body into a prone position, the rifle at high port in both fists as he edged forward across the snow-packed rock, careful lest the snow jutted out further than the rock ledge which supported it, testing each few inches forward that he moved to be certain his weight would be supported.

And he could see now, into the valley.

His ears had not been mistaken. Mechanical noises.

It was something like a halftrack, visible under the half moon which was intermittently above him, one side of it bathed in the orange glow of the campfire which dominated the center of the tents.

There was wood in ample supply here—Rourke had

watched earlier as a team of the Soviet soldiers had used some type of plastique to fell perhaps seven inch diameter pines and then hauled them with ropes toward the center of the camp. Periodically, through the earlier part of the evening, these men or others had put their backs to the logs, shoving them inward to the center of the fire—they would burn through the night and well through into the next night if they were not extinguished, Rourke had surmised.

There was activity near the halftrack, the moonlight combined with the firelight only sufficient to identify shadowy forms that were human, but beyond that, nothing.

But several things could be deduced from the activity nonetheless. It was not an expected visit and it was a visit of some urgency—the shadowy forms did not disappear from the evening's cold into the shelter of any of the tents or the shelter of the halftrack itself.

He saw a light now—some type of flashlight or lantern, but a torch of some type. It seemed to waver about between some of the shadowy forms. A flashlight for reading a map or dispatch—and if it were urgent enough to be read in the night's cold rather than in comfort, it was important.

He continued to watch.

There was more activity—he glanced skyward. The clouds which intermittently obscured the moon were scudding away now on the wind. The light grew more intense.

He brought the SSG to his shoulder, his cheek protected against the synthetic stock by the toque which covered almost his entire face.

He settled the scope on the flashlight beam, then with his left hand slowly stepped up the magnification ring from three power to nine power, holding the image tight and at the center of the reticle to guard against losing it and having to lower magnification and start over again.

He held the image.

And now he could barely make out faces in the firelight and moonlight, forms swathed in heavy cold-weather gear, assault rifles slung from shoulders, the orange light of the fire making the white snow smocks the men of the encampment wore almost demon-like.

The object on which the light was trained was too large for a dispatch—it was a map, Rourke decided.

And a map could mean that Hartman and his German military force were discovered.

There was no way to tell.

But suddenly there was movement in the camp, less than perfectly organized, but clearly a move to break camp.

John Rourke lowered the sniper rifle and rolled back the storm sleeve of his heavy outer garment—the Rolex showed the hour not yet midnight.

"Shit," he murmured.

Natalia—he would have to awaken her.

If the camp was breaking, perhaps to accompany the halftrack-like vehicle, there would be tracks anyone could follow, even in the darkness.

And he had to follow them . . .

The marks of the halftrack in the moon-illumined snow, the footprints of the boots of the soldiers. With Natalia beside him, John Rourke followed them, his body weary from the lack of sleep and the effort it took just to move in this thin air, just to fight off the cold. But he carried Natalia's rifle for her, to make her burdens slightly easier, her pack fully as heavy as his own. He loved her like he had loved no other woman and soon he would lose her. And despite the love for Sarah, despite the child he knew Sarah carried inside her, when Natalia would be gone from him, there would be an emptiness that nothing could fill. Rourke held Natalia's hand and kept walking, after the enemy . . .

The thing which the fire came out of rested in the far corner of the cave. He had watched it for many days. Maur had been the one with courage enough to pick it up, courage enough to bring it to the cave, courage enough to run his gnarled hands over it and keep it as his own. Maur had not the power of speech, but was clever. He, on the other hand, could form sounds which held a shared meaning with those few others like him, and sometimes, when the others were not around, he—Joc—would sit with those like him and they would begin the ritual.

These others in the huge black things which went through the air and had the power of speech, although their sounds were unintelligible to Joc and his soulmates. After the first encounter with the beings who had the things which made fire and were carried along on the air in the huge black things, Joc had determined that it was not that he and the others like him were cursed that they could speak, but that rather this was the natural state of affairs and that Maur, Char and all the others were those who were cursed.

But Joc and few others among all of them could read and to look in the thing which he had so much later learned was called a book was sin and meant death, so he spoke not at all of it, even to those who like him spoke.

The book had a name—he had learned many concepts in the book, and name was one of these. Before, a name had only been a sound by which someone's attention was gotten. But name—it held so much more meaning. There had been a cave, much like this one. Maur had struck him down for speaking and Joc had drawn back to the rear of the cave, hiding from Maur's wrath. He had lain there for some time, this too a concept learned from that which had taught him so much. He had struck his head against something hard and gone to dislodge it—a rock. But it was not a rock. He had later learned that it was a box. He had toyed with the thing for some time, then finally found that the top of the small box opened and inside he had found the book. Pictures, like those some of his people drew on the walls of the caves. And dark lines in regular shapes, the shapes like those in the book which Maur as the leader possessed but could not read but which their tribe had possessed since time had begun. Joc had crept to the front of the cave where there was light in the air and studied from the book. For many periods of light, more than he could reckon. "Spiderman." And this was the first of the words that he learned.

When they had moved to another cave, Joc had left the box behind in secret places and retrieved it each night, then carried it ahead of their line of march, this causing him to have little sleep, but allowing him to keep the book with its words and pictures. Keep Maur from destroying it. He had learned by committing to memory every word and every picture in the book. And he had learned to read the words without the pictures. At night, when Maur squeezed too many of the sleep berries into his mouth, Joc would crawl up to where Maur kept the special book and read it. It was like Spiderman but spoke of other things. A man, Adam and a woman, Eve. Of the making of the earth. Later, much later, it spoke of Jesus.

Because of this reading by the light when it was

night, his eyes had become very bad and he could not see well—at least he assumed this was the cause. One time, Maur had caught him, beaten him and nearly killed him, but not realized he—Joc—had been reading in the special book.

Only one other knew that he read—Jea—his son. His wife, Mur, had known, but like so many, she had gone and was no more.

Maur too had a son—Char—and Char was tall, strong, and evil, like his father. Jea now too could read.

Joc studied the thing which made fire—he was certain it was one of the things called a gun. And when the creatures who used these, men like himself, had used this gun, he had watched and remembered. A box beneath the gun was removable. New boxes could be put in it. A small latch was drawn back to make the gun shoot, and then a small curved piece of metal pulled with the finger. The gun would make much fire or little fire—it was presumably when much fire was made that a new box was used.

Jea lay beside him. And Joc elbowed his son into wakefulness, the boy rubbing his eyes. But he was not a boy, Joc thought, staring at him, rather a man. And Jea too could speak.

The light in the air at night was called the moon, and it was by this light that over the cycle of the seasons he had read, teaching himself. And when there was no moon, he would lie awake at night pondering what the words he read meant. That there had been others like him was abundantly clear, that for some reason his people were little more than wild creatures and other people had devices—he had learned the name of the machines which flew in the air to be helicopters. And they had guns. And they hunted his people and slew his people and those they did not slay they made into slaves and took away.

This cave they stayed in for many full periods of the moon, and they stayed now in caves all around here and did not go far as they had when Joc had had fewer seasons, fewer years, been himself a young man. And so, the box with the book he had buried in a small cave and in the daylight when the sun filled the air he would slip away with Jea and teach the boy. One night, when the moon had filled the air with brightness, he had taken the special book from Maur and Jea had read in it too.

Jea's ability, Joc knew, outshone his own.

He walked silently with Jea, Jea aiding him in the walking as they stepped over the sleeping bodies of the men and women of their tribe, Joc's eyes barely good for seeing in full light these last cycles of the moon.

They left the cave, walking some distance to the flat rocks beside the stream, the moon half full and Jea helping Joc to sit. Joc began to speak. "The moon full-less one more. When Jea be gone?"

Jea spoke. "Jea be gone, father die."

Joc nodded. "Father die—Jea be gone, Jea no be gone."

Jea folded his arms about Joc and Joc folded his arms about Jea. "Jea be gone," Joc said, and beside him, he felt his son's head nod yes . . .

Maria Leuden had emerged from the aircraft changed into desert clothing—but Michael Rourke had not considered it terribly practical. She still wore a skirt, khaki, high waisted, flared or gored or something at the sides—he didn't know the terminology of female attire. And it buttoned at the left side. A plain-looking white shirt, long sleeved but with the sleeves rolled past the elbows, boots which reached to her knees, their tops disappearing beneath the hem of the skirt, her hair bound back with the same silk-looking scarf.

The sun had been fading as they had driven with the young, rather unprepossessing Lieutenant Milton Schmidt, Schmidt's hero-worship of Captain Hammerschmidt ill-disguised, all of them crowded into the Jeep-like vehicle that Hammerschmidt and the other Germans called an SM-4. After some exposure to the nearly non-existent springs of the vehicle, Michael Rourke concluded that the "SM" in the designation stood for sado-masochism. The inventor was the sadist, the persons riding in it the masochists.

As he considered his supposition, he suddenly noticed Maria Leuden glance toward him from the front seat—they had given her presumably the more comfortable spot—and laugh a little with her eyes, then quickly glance away.

Other vehicles followed the SM-4—trucks that looked like the two and one-half ton trucks he had seen in photographs and in films, but halftracks instead and their front tires more balloon-like, more massive.

It had been explained to them by Lieutenant Schmidt that the site used as an airfield had been selected to be sufficiently distant from the base camp that should the arrival of the vertical take-off and landing craft somehow be detected, it would not endanger the security of the base camp itself.

They had stopped once when one of the halftracks developed what turned out to be a minor mechanical difficulty, then proceeded.

According to Common Time by the face of his Rolex, it was well after midnight when they reached the tents of the base camp in a dune-sheltered depression well to the north of the landing area. What had happened to the J-7V aircraft after it had deposited them, he did not know.

The other vehicles broke off, the SM-4 proceeding through the perimeter security—Michael assumed much of it was electronic because there were very few human guards—and stopping before the second largest of the tents.

Hammerschmidt flipped out the rear of the SM-4 to the sand, slapping his hat to his left thigh, tugging off his goggles. Michael removed his goggles as well, as did Maria Leuden—it was the first time he had seen her eyes without the glasses. They were very pretty eyes and he told himself that had it been another time—long distant from now—he would have wanted to look more deeply into them.

He jumped to the sand, perfunctorily helping the archeologist down—she beat her skirt free of sand with the open palms of her hands.

"I would suggest, Herr Captain, Herr Rourke, Fraulein Doctor Leuden, that we take refreshment privately in these quarters I have arranged as the command center."

Hammerschmidt nodded to the junior officer.

Michael Rourke stepped forward. "I'm hungry. Thirsty. Like everybody else. But I want to see that Russian position—how far is it?"

"The Great Pyramid is some fifteen kilometers from our camp, Herr Rourke—but surely—"

"I too share your eagerness, Herr Rourke," Hammerschmidt smiled, "but refreshment seems in order, and the moon—it is too much full for us, I think. We should wait until nearer to dawn. Time will be more critical then, but light more favorable."

Michael nodded, only deferring to Hammerschmidt out of courtesy rather than deference to combat experience—Michael realized that merely by staying

55

alive in that time of his boyhood between the Night of
The War and the Great Conflagration, he was more
experienced than any living man—except his father,
except Paul Rubenstein—except Vladmir Karamatsov.

"Very well," he said softly.

Maria Leuden spoke. "We will be working in the
desert here—and our bodies will be ill-suited to it—
but through my research, I have prepared for this as
best I could. While we refresh ourselves, I can brief
you."

The obvious thought crossed his mind. Maria
Leuden's eyes flashed toward him behind her round-
rimmed glasses, then away.

He had seen the look before—in the Jeep-like SM-
4, and seen the look in the eyes of his sister.

In his sister, he could accept it—in this woman, he
did not.

"All right—I'm starving," he announced, starting
into the tent after Hammerschmidt, the Lieutenant
stepping back and opening the tent flap.

He had seen the film, "Lawrence of Arabia," and
the other films which depicted the vastness of the
Middle Eastern Desert. He had read books depicting
the Bedouin life. But nothing had prepared him for
the interior of the tent.

It was air conditioned, hermetically sealed it
seemed from the desert, the ambient temperature
almost chilling, despite the drastic drop of desert heat
as the sun had declined. A table dominated the center
of the tent—long, narrow, studded with camp chairs.

Enlisted personnel brought in several duffle bag-
like sacks Michael had seen removed from the aircraft, seen transferred from the helicopter which had
taken them out of Iceland.

As other enlisted personnel brought forth food and

what appeared to be wine—Michael tasted and confirmed that indeed it was, but a trifle sweet for his palate. Maria Leuden with Lieutenant Schmidt's help began opening and unpacking the bags. "The greatest danger in the desert climate is the sun and its effect on the body—stating the obvious," she began, not smiling. "The Arabs guarded against this in several ways, but chiefly in shielding the body from the extremes, reducing the effect of these extremes upon the body. I have had prepared clothing similar to that worn by the Arabs in similar situations."

Hammerschmidt lit one of the non-carcinogenic cigarettes. Michael sipped at his wine—he wondered if it were non-alcoholic.

"The keffiyeh shields the head and the neck. The top of the head is the most susceptible portion of the body to heat loss and gain, except in some cases, I believe—there are medical data—"

"Is," Michael corrected unconsciously—

"Either is correct, since data is the plural form," she nodded, not smiling.

Michael nodded back.

"At any event, for protracted periods of time in the desert, our health will best be served to take advantage of the knowledge gained by the Arabs over the centuries. For each of us that will comprise the team, I have had prepared a keffiyeh," and she produced a large-seeming square of off-white material of what appeared to Michael's untrained eye to be a loose weave. "The keffiyeh is held in place by this headband which was called an akal." It was made of various strands of cord running parallel to each other with large, knot-like objects—she held the headband to her own forehead, the knots at roughly the temples. "And," she said, setting down the akal and drawing now from one of the other duffle bags, "for each of us there is a jellaba. The robe. It may appear heavy and is made of wool, but it is this very heaviness which controls moisture loss from the body and shields the body from heat. It is loose and after a time you'll find it comfortable. It can be worn open," and she slipped it on, "or closed against the cold. And the desert at night and in the hours before dawn can be quite cold."

Michael sipped again at his wine—he'd come for more important things than a costume party . . .

Paul Rubenstein sat bolt upright—his right hand reached to the bed; Annie was not beside him. There was no light from the bathroom. He pushed down the covers, throwing his feet over the side of the bed, the rug feeling cool to his naked flesh. "Annie?"

There was no answer—in the darkness which was never total in the room, the white shadow of the large nursing shawl she used like a robe was missing from the chest at the foot of the bed. Paul Rubenstein found his Levis and skinned into them, then found the long sleeved, dark blue cotton sweater he had worn earlier over a shirt and pulled it on now, shirtless as he stuffed his bare feet into his slippers.

From beside the bed, he picked up the battered Browning High Power, stuffing it into the waistband of his pants, pulling the sweater down over it.

There were no keys necessary—nothing else really. He left the room, closing the door into the hall of the dormitory behind him, walking along the length of the corridor as silently as he could because of the hour.

He reached the end of the corridor and stepped through the double doors onto the small porch which fronted the steps leading down toward the gardens which gave way to the central mall of the Hekla village. Annie sat, swathed in her shawl, on one of the massive stone facades which flanked the steps.

From the height of the steps, Paul called to her. "Hey—can I join you?"

She turned around, as though startled, he thought, smiling up at him. "Uh—huh—I'm sorry—I didn't mean to wake you up." But he was already starting down the steps toward her, crossed to the stone on which she sat, then dropped down beside her. "I just—ahh—"

"What's wrong?" he asked her.

"I saw it, Paul—I dreamed that Madison was hurt, was dying—and I woke up to the gunshots."

"Aww, Annie," and he embraced her, holding her tight.

"I—ahh—I saw it. And I dreamed again tonight. I don't wanna dream—I don't wanna, Paul—it's a curse. I can see—things that are happening far away—"

"Remote viewing, they call it—ahh—"

"The library?"

"Yeah," he nodded, hearing Annie sniffle against his chest, smelling her hair, his lips touching her forehead. "What did you see?"

"Daddy and Natalia. They were walking across the snow, following some depressions in the snow. But something was going to happen to them—and Natalia was very cold—and—"

"And what, sweetheart?"

"And—somewhere ahead of them—I couldn't see clearly and I knew that they couldn't see it at all—but there was something horrible. Death—I could feel it," and her body trembled against him and he held her more tightly. "I—Jesus, Paul—I—"

"We can't break radio silence—but we might be able to go after them. Your father should know anyway about Madison. Breaking radio silence might get them in worse trouble, ya know?"

"Uh-huh," she whispered.

"All right. Listen—you get some things packed. Cold weather gear. Get the weapons ready. I'll go see Major Volkmer at the base—and if that doesn't swing it, I'll get Doctor Munchen out of bed. Somehow, we'll set it up. All right?"

"I love you," she whispered.

He had nearly gotten the purple quality of the light to the point where he didn't really notice it. But he noticed it now, noticed the warmth of the night there in the heart of the dormant Icelandic volcano. He could smell the flowers and the plants. He could smell the woman smell of Annie, his wife.

"I love you," Paul Rubenstein whispered, holding her for one moment longer . . .

Doctor Munchen lit a cigarette. Major Volkmer was saying, "I hardly think, Herr Rubenstein, that the dreams of an impressionable young woman who has just suffered traumatic shock are sufficient cause to dispatch a military expedition into hostile territory, an expedition whose very arrival might trigger the danger she so fears for her father."

Volkmer was a short man, his body one obviously developed through building, his shirt open at the collar, otherwise compacted to his torso; muscles rippled there as he paced the room. His dark eyes seemed to be looking through the walls of Munchen's office, looking at no one as he ran his stubby-fingered hands through his thinning blond hair.

Munchen spoke now. "Prior to the Night of The War, both the Soviet Union and the United States were actively engaged in researching the practical military applications of certain phenomena in the field of parapsychology, among these what Herr Rubenstein has referred to as remote viewing. There were some remarkably interesting results. Certain remote viewers with the proper stimulus could reveal details later verified by satellite and high altitude observation photography, details of missile installations and the like.

"Annie—ahh—she has—whether it's a gift or a curse. Before Sarah or Natalia or John or myself were awakened back at The Retreat, she saw Michael in danger. And she awakened us. If she hadn't, Michael would have been dead."

"Coincidence?" Major Volkmer smiled as he shrugged his shoulders.

"Agreed—possible. Natalia told me that she could almost feel something probing her mind for an experience she'd had years before where she had used a knife to kill a man who was trying to—ahh—attack her. Anyway—Annie, ahh—Annie—"

"Killed the American traitor, Blackburn," Munchen supplied. "In exactly the same manner. Frau Rubenstein has conversed with me since the death of her sister-in-law."

"She saw Madison being shot—then awakened when the gunfire awakened us all." Paul fell silent, eyeing Munchen's cigarette, wishing that he still smoked.

Munchen sat on the edge of his desk. "The Rourkes are extraordinarily gifted in intelligence. That is readily apparent to anyone. Sarah, the wife of the Herr Doctor Rourke. Her intelligence seems extraordinary. Combining the genes of the Herr Doctor Rourke and his frau—the possibilities exist. Couple this with the totally unknown effects of nearly five centuries of the mind functioning at a level of activity

61

about which we know nothing. Could five centuries of development in a person of tremendous intellectual potential have achieved the crossing of a barrier? Hmm? With the adults, it was difficult, I think. But with the children, the mind was fertile, raw material. It is likely that if Frau Rubenstein possesses this ability, young Michael may possess it as well. But the female—there is greater incidence of special psychic awareness among women, and women to listen more easily, less reluctantly to their emotions, their feelings. Michael might well have such dreams and not even be aware of them. But Annie Rourke Rubenstein is aware of them."

Volkmer leaned heavily against the wall of the office. "You believe, then, Herr Doctor, that I should co-operate?"

"It is my official recommendation, Herr Major."

"How can you gamble otherwise?" Paul Rubenstein asked. "If John and Natalia and Captain Hartman are lost, we're at square one finding the Soviet Underground City, aren't we? And you don't have enough forces to defend your homeland in Argentina, the Eden Project Base Camp and the Icelandic Communities if Karamatsov should throw all his weight against one target. But if we can destroy his base, his source of supply—"

"Herr Rubenstein," Volkmer began, pushing himself away from the wall and crossing the room, standing at the apex of a triangle formed by Munchen, Rubenstein and himself. "Though you are not biologically a Rourke, you reason like one. Perhaps it is contagious? Hmm?" And Volkmer started to laugh.

Chapter Seven

The Great Pyramid had survived—somehow Michael Rourke had known that it would. Maria Leuden brushed past him, to peer over the rift of sand. "Mein Gott," she murmured.

"I thought religion was something rather new to you folks," Michael whispered to her.

"It is an expression, Herr Rourke."

"Ahh—gotchya," Michael told her. He looked along the ridge line formed by the sand—Hammerschmidt, in his Arab mufti, along with the sergeant and the five other German commandoes, were positioned along its length, a heavy machinegun set up on its bipod.

Michael sank below the level of the dune, staring back into the desert through which they had come—fifteen kilometers from the site of the German camp. The stars' brilliance was slightly diminished here—the yellow glow of the Soviet worklights saw to that.

Maria Leuden hugged the jellaba close around her, her head and neck swathed in a woolen shawl. "It was built during The Old Kingdom—but we don't really know much about the people who built it, really. The priest and historian, Manetho—some of his works survive in bits and snatches but as recounted by persons living at least six centuries after he wrote. It was begun nearly two and one-half millenia before the birth of Christ. Why would this man Karamatsov—"

"Hide a weapon here?"

"But don't you see—by some accounts the Pyramid may be vastly older than that. No one has ever really explored what may be inside it—not completely."

Michael rolled onto his stomach and elbowed his way to the ridgeline again, this time taking the borrowed German binoculars up from their strap around his neck, placing them to his eyes. They were electronic, allowing precise range measurement, precise measurement of object in view. He pushed the button for automatic focusing, releasing the button when the focusing was corrected to his vision. "At the base," he heard her telling him, "each side averages slightly over seven hundred seventy-five feet—the height is four hundred eight-one feet—the Pyramid's exact dimensions were—"

"A subject of great debate—I know. The four sides aren't exactly equal, but rather seem to have been designed to reflect precise measurements of terrestrial geography—" He could see men moving about the Pyramid of Cheops, digging with hand tools. "Do you believe in the concepts of good and evil?"

"What?"

He put down the binoculars and slid closer to her down the embankment, staring into her eyes through her glasses. "Do you believe in good and evil—that they complement one another. Without one we could not perceive the other?"

"Yes—I think so—but, Herr Rourke."

"Fraulein Doctor—I've thought about Vladmir Karamatsov for quite some time on and off, and quite steadily since his suicide squad caused the death of my wife and child. To kill someone who is very hard to kill, it's important, I think, to know that person. To

64

know that person in as great detail as possible. There was little detail available beyond that which I already knew. Natalia—Major Tiemerovna—could have provided more. As his wife, she probably knows him better than anyone. But Natalia was unavailable to me. Instead, then, I carefully considered every fact I had, from as many different perspectives as I could. I came to the conclusion that in his way, Marshal Karamatsov is the antithesis of my father, and I suppose of me as well since everyone tells me I'm very like my father. Now, if we assume that what the Rourke family has fought for all these years—centuries really—is the objective good, then it's easy to concede that Vladmir Karamatsov is the objective evil. But persons who are diametrically opposed may have astounding similarities, perhaps be so thoroughly opposed to each other because of these similarities. A similarity I have found in my father and Vladmir Karamatsov is a simple and basic one. They are both fastidious planners, and both totally committed to succeeding in their goals. My dad—he was totally committed to survival, but not at the cost of integrity. But on the other hand, Karamatsov was totally committed to survival at any cost, having no integrity at all. And, unlike my father, if he couldn't win the game, he would destroy the arena. So we have assumed he is looking for some fantastic weapon. Maybe some super bomb—who knows. But if you expected all life on earth to perhaps cease, but that somehow you would make it through, and if you wanted some sort of special thing to be waiting for you centuries into the future, what would you do?"

"Put that thing—whatever it was—in the most secure place I could."

"Not just secure—but findable. Consider this. Coastline could change. Mountains could be blasted away, new ones could rise in their stead. The poles could have changed so drastically that compass coordinates would be useless. You wouldn't want a place that could conceivably be covered, obscured—by snow or water or vegetation. All he's using the Great Pyramid for, Fraulein Doctor, is a landmark. What he wants is buried out there in the desert. What his men are doing is digging away to the base so the measurements would be precise. He has coordinates and he could likely follow them to the exact spot. But like my father, he's planning ahead—just in case. Notice," and he jerked his thumb over the dune and toward the Pyramid, "they're only digging away at two corners. He'll shoot an azimuth that's pre-determined precisely off each corner. Where the two lines intersect is where the object—whatever it is—is buried. Surveyors instruments. All the right equipment. He'll find it. Very soon. No matter how much sand has accumulated over it throughout the centuries, he'll go to the exact spot, know exactly where it is and order the digging begun."

"We should—"

"Should we now," Michael smiled. "Let him find it? Probably. But we should be in a position to immediately prevent its use. And that's dubious. So we have to find it first ourselves and be waiting for him when he arrives. He has the digging equipment—we don't. Use the binoculars and look under those tarps to the west—"

She crawled past him, to the ridge, taking her own binoculars.

"Careful so they don't see you, Fraulein."

"Earth moving equipment."

"Yes," Michael nodded.

"But—"

"Whatever it is, it can't be buried too terribly far

off into the desert or they would have air dropped the equipment nearer to the site—it's not really needed here."

"Then it should be something they'll find very rapidly once—"

"Yes, once they reach the base of the Pyramid," Michael Rourke completed for her. "So—any suggestions?"

She slid down across the sand toward him.

She smiled strangely. "Why do you ask me?"

"All right, let me ask you something else. Can you read everybody all the time, part of the time, just some people, how does it work?"

Maria Leuden looked away—and he thought that her face seemed to flush with color—but in the starlight and the half moon it was difficult to tell. It could only have been shadow. "I—ahh—only some people."

"Anything special about that I should know?"

"No, not that you should know."

"Well—all right—have either of us had any good thoughts about what to do here?"

"You have—you want to penetrate the camp down there, see if you can locate the coordinates and get the approximate location so we can be waiting for Karamatsov when he arrives. You have told yourself you won't kill him yet—not until he leads us to the weapon. And you are angry with yourself for doing that."

"Then you can read my thoughts all the time." And he looked at her.

"Michael—I mean—"

"Tell me what I thought."

"I don't want to—to tell you."

"All right," and he looked away.

Maria Leuden began to talk to him. "When I was

67

in my studies, some of the ones with me who were in the Youth, bridging into the SS—there was this boy."

Michael looked at her.

"You are going to make me tell you, aren't you?"

"No. Never mind."

"But I really want to tell you—and I don't know why. They—ahh—this boy and some of his friends. He name was Fritz. And Fritz tried to—and, ahh—I scratched his face badly. He surprised me in my room and I was shaving my legs—I used the razor. Across his face. He ran away."

Michael simply looked at her, saying nothing.

"You are wondering what happened then—how does that—"

"Yes, I was. But you don't have to—"

"I know that too." She took off her glasses and pushed the shawl back from her hair. "With some of his friends—he came for me. I didn't report him to the authorities—his father was very important in the SS. Ahh—they came for me. It was the weekend. I wasn't expected anywhere until Monday. They beat me—only to stop me screaming I think. They put tape over my mouth then. Fritz was studying medicine and he injected me. Afterward, I found out they injected me seven times. This drug was an hallucinogen. So my mind was someplace else. If there is a God—well, I thank God for that. Even his father's influence couldn't save him. Fritz and the others were arrested, tried. Fritz was killed during your father's assault on the Complex. He was one of the SS men torturing Frau Stern. The drugs addicted me. It took months for me to recover, the residual effect of the drug having somehow altered the chemical balance of my brain—at least that is what the doctors said. But while I was recovering, it started. I could tell the thoughts of the young man I was engaged to marry. I

68

could read the thoughts of my father, a professor at the university. I could read the thoughts of my girl friend, Elsie. Elsie became a chemical engineer. There was an accident—a spill. Her body was destroyed by acid. I could feel her death. My father died of his third heart attack—I could feel his pain when he died. I was in a coma for almost a week after it. And the young man I was intended to. After I recovered from the attack and the effect of the drugs. He—ahh—he couldn't live with the thought of a woman who had been—used. He took his own life. There was no pain. He—he—"

Michael folded his arms about her and she leaned her head against his chest.

"That's—that is why—I was afraid when I found I could read your thoughts."

Michael looked down at her. "Read my thoughts now. Tell me my thoughts."

She looked up at him, the corners of her eyes wet with tears, tears flooding over the rims, streaming down her cheeks. "That I should not be afraid. That you won't die. That you are a Rourke. And so I should believe you."

"Yes," Michael Rourke whispered . . .

He had crossed along the ridge, Hammerschmidt accompanying him, the sergeant in command of the other five enlisted personnel, Maria Leuden with them.

Hammerschmidt had stripped away the Arab mufti, the sleeves of his shirt rolled up past his elbows, bareheaded, one of the German pistols in his right fist, one of the German assault rifles tight slung to his back.

Michael had left his leather jacket behind and his

rifle, only the two Beretta pistols in their shoulder holsters under his arms, the four-inch model 629 .44 Magnum in the flap holster at his right hip.

But in his right fist was the Life Support System II knife given him by the old swordmaker, Michael's fingers bunched tight to it.

His palms sweated a bit.

The moon was nearly down. In less than an hour it would be dawn.

They had reached the end of the ridge of sand, the Great Pyramid looming high above them now, what ravages there had been of time unnoticeable to Michael as he compared the reality of the Pyramid to his mental images of it.

Michael dropped into a crouch, the nearest of the Soviet guards a few meters away, his back turned to them.

Hammerschmidt gestured to himself, then to the guard. Michael shook his head. He gestured to the guard, then gestured with his knife.

Hammerschmidt nodded.

Michael was up, moving, slowly, his eyes flickering from side to side lest he be detected, his mind focusing on the image of the Pyramid to avoid giving the guard the sixth sense warning his father, John Rourke, had often spoken of.

He kept moving, gradually increasing his pace, the knife held like a rapier in his right fist.

Less distance now than the span of his arm, Michael leaped forward, his left hand going over the guard's mouth and chin, snapping the head back, his right arm arcing around the guard's body, thrusting the knife in deep and downward—the blade was long enough to pass through the body and exit. But he drove it downward through the throat and into the chest, the body weight of the Soviet trooper sagging against him now, Michael giving the blade a twist as he withdrew it, letting the body sink into the sand.

He glanced back—Hammerschmidt was already running up to join him.

With Hammerschmidt's help, Michael dragged the body up and into the depression beyond the edge of the ridgeline.

The nearest wall of the Pyramid—the girl had gotten him thinking in meters and he normally thought in yards. A hundred yards, men digging at the corner at the far edge of the wall.

Michael licked his lips. He gestured with his head toward Hammerschmidt, then toward the wall of the Pyramid.

Hammerschmidt nodded as Michael stabbed the Life Support System II into the sand to clean it of blood.

Michael broke into a run, at a right angle to the position where the Russian had stood, for the near wall of the Pyramid. He ran flat out, cover unavailable, finding running easier here than at Hekla, the air more dense here.

He threw himself against the wall, flat, Hammerschmidt beside him a second later.

The German commando leader hissed, "Herr Rourke—we should cross behind the Pyramid I think."

Michael nodded only, taking off again at a dead run along the length of the wall, the running slow here, the sand softer. He slowed still more as he reached the corner of the Pyramid, edging toward it now, the knife sheathed, the 629 in his right fist from the leather.

He could feel Hammerschmidt behind him as he edged ever so slightly around the corner of the massive structure. No one was visible.

Michael looked back—they had not been noticed—yet. Nor had the absence of the guard—yet. He rounded the corner and ran along the next wall of the Pyramid now, the revolver holstered again, his hands weaponless. It was darker here, away from the glare of the yellow worklights, but the dark a grayblue—very soon now the sun would rise.

As he ran, he heard voices, then slowed himself. He had taught himself Russian from tapes, practiced it with Natalia, worked with Russian instructional tapes at Hekla in off moments. He could understand it well enough—someone was talking with a superior officer. And one of the voices—somehow inside himself, he felt it was Karamatsov.

More slowly now he kept moving, but his hands moved automatically, ripping the two Beretta 92 SB-Fs from the leather beneath his armpits.

He could hear the telltale sound of Hammerschmidt unholstering his pistol.

Michael's thumbs edged up the ambidexterous safeties as he moved ahead, the Russian voices loud enough to clearly make out conversation now—"Comrade Marshal, it should be a matter of less than an hour."

"Tell the men to dig more rapidly. I wish to be out of here, have what we came for."

"But Comrade Marshal Karamatsov—I do not—"

"Major Krakovski, have you considered that we might lose our historic struggle?"

"Comrade Marshal!"

Michael stopped, a few yards back from the corner where the walls met, in his mind's eye seeing Karamatsov and the one called Major Krakovski, just beyond the juncture of the walls.

He waited.

Karamatsov, his voice strange sounding, spoke

again. "We had anticipated the Eden Project alone surviving from the world before. But no. The Germans in what was Argentina, now allies of the Eden Project fleet, allies of the Icelandic communities, the allies of Rourke. Mankind was more adaptable than any of us could have imagined. In a battle of concentrated military might, warfare between ourselves and the Germans and their allies might continue for decades unless we were to utilize the few thermonuclear devices still remaining to us. And if we fail to crush them with these devices, what would remain? Even if we were triumphant, hum? Could the atmosphere sustain the shock of a second nuclear war?"

"I—"

"I had prepared for this possibility. An ultimate weapon," and he laughed. "I shall retire to my tent. When the diggers have reached the foundation level, prepare the transits for the sightings. I shall personally confirm their accuracy. Then we shall recover our prize."

"Comrade Marshal—"

"Major, it will be all right," the voice of Karamatsov almost whispered.

Michael edged forward again, his fists tightening on the butts of his pistols. He could step around the corner, kill Karamatsov now.

This weapon—what was it? If Karamatsov were dead, would Karamatsov's underlings be able to find it, use it?

If he—Michael Rourke—opened fire now, he would kill Karamatsov, but himself be killed. Hammerschmidt as well, Maria Leuden and the others. And what little intelligence had been gleaned concerning Karamatsov's quest here in the desert would be lost.

He raised both pistols, working the safeties down into the "safe" position.

Michael Rourke closed his eyes.

He felt Hammerschmidt's hand on his shoulder.

Without opening his eyes, Michael nodded.

There would be another time.

He turned, opening his eyes, breaking into a jog trot along the wall in the direction from which he had come. They would take the body with them and bury it in the sand where Karamatsov's force would never find the hapless guard. Let Karamatsov assume what he liked as to the sentry's fate.

Already, he was forming a plan, a method—observe the engineers when they took the sightings with their transits, calculate the angle of the telescopes and shoot back azimuths to locate the intersection point. It would be approximate only—but it would get them there.

He reached the next corner—it was clear around the corner—no alert.

Michael Rourke kept running.

Chapter Eight

Jea clutched the thing which made fire—he remembered how one of his kind had taken a rock and smashed in the head of the one in black who came from the helicopter and taken it.

The gun.

Jea ran.

Maur or Char would take life for this and Jea was not really certain if the gun would make fire for him as it made fire for the one in black who was dead.

When the snow had come, the cold had come out of the air as well, and smoke formed on his breath as he ran. Along with the gun, he carried with him the book with the pictures from which he had learned to tell words, the book inside its casket that felt cold to the touch like parts of the gun felt. Would that he could sling a web, like the one in the book, and move from tree to tree.

He wondered—the one in the book. Were there really tall places like that in the years ago? Were all the people who lived inside the tall things with the spots that held the strange water in the walls?

Jea looked back behind him.

It was not Maur, but Maur's son, Char—and Char was running. Jea could hear the sounds of Char's rage now, the screams. In Char's hand was the club. It was not made from one of the trees with needles—were they cedars? It was made from another tree which had no needles and it was strong enough to break bodies when it fell.

And Char waved the club over his head and screamed.

Jea, his feet numbing with the cold, ran, holding the gun . . .

John Rourke let Natalia sag against him, his eyes studying the tracks in the gray orange glow from the horizon. As the pre-dawn hours had worn on, there were fewer and fewer tracks of the foot soldiers, more of them with each opportunity, he surmised, clambering aboard the armored personnel carrier out of weariness, sacrificing the warming exercise of movement for respite from exhaustion.

Ahead, the tracks veered off, out of the chain of valleys through which they moved and along a gently rising defile.

He estimated that if the Russians had continued to travel, they would be by now at least four hours ahead. But his goal was not to catch them, but to follow them.

He looked at Natalia. His decision was made. Once they came up out of the valley and onto the ridgeline, he would find a suitable place, erect one of the climatically controlled tents and give her time to rest.

There was no choice, her well-being more important to him than satisfying his curiosity.

"Come on, Natalia—just a little while further."

"I'm fine, John—really I am."

"Sure," and he smiled, helping her along, flanking the tracks on the right as he had done ever since taking up after the Russians.

Why had the Russians folded camp and left in the middle of the night? Few things in any army ever made obvious good sense, he knew—but why? They walked on, the sun winking above and below the peaks along the horizon as they moved and shifted their perspective, but the light less gray now, more a pale, washed out yellow.

And as the sun rose, the wind which had been all but non-existent, heightened, a breeze gentle enough but cold, gusting occasionally and penetrating the body like a knife when it did. His own body was beyond weariness, on an adrenaline high, he realized, a high from which he might crash soon into exhaustion.

As his eyes scanned the tracks on the ground, he saw something else. A footprint unlike all the others, as though moccasined and yet not.

"What is that, John?"

"I don't know—can you stand?"

"Yes."

John Rourke took his arm from around her waist and dropped to one knee in the snow. The sun was up over the peak directly opposite them now and he could see the ground a little more clearly. Whatever the footgear, it was clearly the footprint of a man, a man running.

Rourke rose at his full height now, tiredness forgotten for the instant. His eyes peered into the grayness—another footprint and another, and a similar track, only slightly larger, partially obscured one of the originals.

"Two men running, either away from something or chasing each other. The footgear though."

Natalia stood beside him, a small flashlight in her left hand, its beam aimed toward the snow. "That is not Russian. Or German."

"No—there's somebody else out here."

"That's impossible, John—I think—I don't know."

John Rourke nodded only. He wanted a cigar but not badly enough to remove his gloves and open his coat to get one.

Rourke instead told Natalia, "Shut off the flashlight. Let's follow these a while if you're up to it."

"All right," she whispered.

Rourke looked at her. "You sure?"

"I'm sure."

He nodded, then started ahead, following the footprints slightly higher into the rocks now, the lead prints and ones pursuing—it had to be that—veering off left, in the same general direction as the tracks of the Soviet APC. The lead tracks were becoming more erratic now, the pursuing tracks longer strided than before—whoever was chasing the first person was getting closer, Rourke surmised.

A fall—a hasty movement to get up—running on.

Rourke hissed to Natalia. "Your PPK/S with the silencer—get it out."

"Yes."

Rourke reached to his right hip for the Python, easing it slowly from the leather, moving ahead more slowly now. The tracks rose along a ridgeline within the ridgeline they now followed.

John Rourke froze in his tracks—a sound, a sound like something he hadn't heard for five centuries. Animal—almost. A scream like something wounded.

Natalia stepped closer to him.

Looking at her for an instant, Rourke isolated the sound as it came again, the shock of hearing it so great that the direction of its origin hadn't registered with him the first time.

He broke into a dead run across the snow, Natalia behind him, running in the snowshoes never easy, but more difficult because of the unevenness of the terrain, running along an embankment's course, then up.

Rourke stopped. Two men nearly naked, their skins rough and leathery, their bodies strangely non-human, but very human, clad in strips of bark woven into ill-fitting tunics. One of them was powerfully built, the other slight of build, but wiry—they were locked in what had to be combat to the death, both men grasping, fighting over a Russian assault rifle.

"Here—" And Rourke stabbed the Python toward Natalia, taking the PPK/S from her right fist, half skidding, half running down the snow-covered embankment.

No silencer was perfectly soundless—this one on the PPK/S wasn't either. Rourke fired the pistol into the ground between the feet of the two men, both of them jumping back, Rourke's eyes tracking the assault rifle—it was in the hands of the larger of the two men. Rourke worked the PPK/S's safety to drop the hammer and tossed the gun airborne, "Natalia!"

Only amateurs or fools in movies threw guns around, especially loaded ones—amateurs or fools or people too desperate to have the time to do anything else.

Rourke launched himself forward, diving for the midsection of the bigger of the two men, Rourke's left shoulder impacting the wall of muscle that was the man's chest and abdomen, the assault rifle flying from the big man's hands into the snow.

He could hear the pop of Natalia's silenced pistol again—there was no time to look to see why. The big man's fists hammered down across Rourke's back, Rourke not letting go, his gloved hands welding to the big man's hips, Rourke throwing his weight left and down, the big man going down with him, Rourke on top.

He caught a whiff of breath—it was foul. Rourke's right fist snaked upward, into position and then laced the big man across the jaw.

Rourke felt his knuckles almost break.

The head he'd struck snapped back, the teeth bared now, a hand crushing at Rourke's throat, a hand with a grip like a bench vise.

Rourke's right knee smashed up—if it was human and he was sure it was, then it had to have testicles—the big man howled as Rourke's knee impacted and Rourke felt the squish of flesh. The man's left hand grabbed at Rourke's chest, closed over a handful of arctic gear and Rourke was airborne, crashing down into the snow, rolling, but awkwardly because of the snowshoes.

The big man was up, doubled half forward, Rourke to his feet, breathing hard—the big man charged like a bull. Rourke sidestepped, wanting to kick, unable to do so with the snowshoes, instead launching his full body weight against the man's right side in a slam, hurtling the bigger man down. Rourke's right elbow snapped back, into the side of the head, then again into the neck. Rourke came to his knees now, balling both fists together and clubbing them downward and across the man's jawline, the knife edges of both hands together tight like the business end of a sledge-hammer.

The big man's body sagged—to be on the safe side, Rourke rolled back and away, grabbing for the Gerber MkII at his belt. No pistol was near enough, the rifles lost in the snow as he'd first dove toward the man.

"I have him covered, John."

Rourke edged back on his knees along the snow, climbed to his feet. He sheathed the Gerber as he looked around.

Natalia smiled—he couldn't see her mouth for the scarf which covered most of her face, the sparkle in her blue eyes all that showed the smile at all. "His name is Jea—and he speaks a kind of French that sounds like what you Americans used to call Hog Latin."

"Pig Latin," Rourke automatically corrected. And he looked at the slighter of the two men, at the woven bark clothing, the bark strip footgear. "Enchante," John Rourke bowed. "Je suis John Rourke, mon ami."

The man smiled—sort of.

Chapter Nine

Michael Rourke had gotten no sleep.

The keffiyeh had been a good idea, the sun already hot and not mid-morning yet. He lay prone on a ridge of dune more than a half mile distant from the Great Pyramid, Doctor Maria Leuden surprisingly durable enough to be beside him. Michael Rourke had used a bayonet fitted German assault rifle stabbed into the sand as a "tent pole" and used the jellaba as a lean-to rather than a robe, huddled under it except for the portion of his head and hands needed for using his binoculars, huddled under it with Maria Leuden. Michael Rourke's eyes studied the surveyor's transit at the left side of the wall of the Pyramid which faced him.

"They're about ready to put it into position."

"I hope they hurry—it is very hot."

Michael Rourke looked away from the binoculars and at Maria Leuden beside him. "I'm sorry if I'm a little abrupt."

"I understand it is a family trait."

"Touche," he smiled. "But—well—we've been

fighting this war longer than you and your people. This thing with Karamatsov—it's not a military action to us—to me. It's a personal thing. He's almost killed my father and mother and sister and Paul Rubenstein and what he's done to his wife—death is too good for him. What he did to my wife—"

"And to you."

"You mean gut shooting me and leaving me to bleed to death?"

"I don't mean that—not that."

Michael looked away, through the binocular tubes, focusing one level of his attention on the surveyor's transit he watched. Captain Otto Hammerschmidt would be watching the other one. Another level of his consciousness focused on Maria Leuden's words. "He's robbed you of the only personal life you've ever known. You were always dislocated from humanity—that is clear. I have read our data on the Rourke family. Forced to be an adult from your earliest childhood, forced to be responsible, to be competent. Never a chance to release, to be off guard. And then finally, that one night—you let your guard down a little. Or you believe that at least—and your wife and unborn baby were killed."

Without looking at her, he almost whispered, "I see that you and Doctor Munchen took the same correspondence course in psychiatry—"

"Correspondence? Course?"

"Through the mail—but you don't have any mail, do you? I got mail when I was a little kid. Christmas cards and birthday cards from relatives. And I bought some books at school once and I wound up on a mailing list for somebody and I used to get stuff mailed to me that you'd just look at and throw away. My mother told me there were things called junk mail—things mailed to you that you didn't want to bother reading but the mailman had to deliver anyway and you'd just throw them in the wastebasket unopened. But now there isn't any mail at all."

"Do you remember what it was like to be a child?"

Michael closed his eyes. "Yeah—we rode horseback a lot, and sometimes it was cold, and sometimes it was raining and lots of times Momma wouldn't eat because she'd tell us she wasn't hungry and after a while I realized it wasn't that—just that the food was running low. There was a dog I played with on a farm, but the farm was attacked by madmen and there was fire and I was using a rifle a lot and I killed people and this older woman there—she screamed a lot. And I learned a lot about the human body—I saw human bodies bleed after I shot into them or stabbed a knife into them. And I never got frightened of seeing dead people, because I saw so many of them. I saw dogs fighting over half-rotted human arms and legs. So—ahh—"

"You are hiding from me. Why?"

"I don't know what you mean."

"You are attracted to me—as I am to you. But you feel that your wife has just died and to allow yourself to feel anything for me would be wrong somehow. True?"

"I don't know." And mercifully, they began to adjust the surveyor's transit. "Look—they're getting ready." He had learned while watching the Germans building their base outside Mt. Hekla in Iceland that a surveyor's transit was no longer as simple a device as it had been in the books of which he had first heard of the device, as it had been in films where he had seen one employed. His father had a transit and John Rourke had used it to lay out the garden plot outside the Retreat. It had seemed a needless formality to Michael at the time, but he realized now that his father had been trying to whet his or Annie's appetite to learn its use. Michael had obliged. So had Annie.

But these devices used no ordinary light and no simple eyeballing of measurement—if the Soviet transits were like those used by the Germans, and outwardly they appeared to be, they emitted a measured beam of laser light and for an operation such as this, where two transits would be used to locate an exact spot, each transit would give a diode readout for precise distance and when the beams crossed, give the readout at the nexus of the beams. Using such a system, their potential for error was slightly less than a centimeter at a mile, again judging by the German counterparts.

He had first intended to monitor the positions of the transit, but had in the moments just after dawn devised a still better plan. Mortars were in place that would fire smoke rounds on cue and near the mortars but not too near were German transits, remotely operated which would lock onto the nexus of the Russian transit beams and pinpoint the exact spot for the Germans.

There would be a small show of force by German gunships, then the gunships would flee to the south, a direction that would lead any Soviet pursuit craft away from the German camp and the location of whatever it was Karamatsov had come here to the desert to find.

Lieutenant Milton Schmidt would lead this element, even picking up the mortar crews just to add icing to the cake, hopefully giving the illusion that the smoke was preparation for a hit and run attack. If the secondary laser beams of the German transits were sighted, the ruse might be discovered. But there was a more than substantial chance they would not be.

After the skirmish, with the Germans in withdrawal, Karamatsov would be free to seek out his prize with even greater urgency since there was a verifiable enemy presence.

A voice in his ear through the radio set he wore, the earpiece leading up from the radio unit at his belt. "Ready," the voice of Otto Hammerschmidt came through.

"Ready," Michael whispered, taking the set from his belt, depressing the push-to-talk button and whispering in it.

There was the possibility that the Russians would have heard the transmissions—but even if they had, it would be unlikely they would have the time to act.

Michael Rourke had learned that life was not a gamble, but a carefully calculated risk—he could not recall his father ever putting it that way, but it was the way his father lived.

Michael reached up to the rifle, the rifle propping the jellaba over them against the sun. He tugged the sheathed bayonet free of the material, the jellaba collapsing over them.

He rolled onto his back, squinting against the indirect light of the sun.

He removed the bayonet from the rifle and handed the bayonet to Maria Leuden. "Here—have a knife. Have a rifle as a matter of fact." He shrugged into the jellaba and refocused the binoculars across the sand, toward the Great Pyramid. The laser transits were emitting light in the red, intermittently.

He could see flashes, like bloodied shadows as vagrant gusts of wind would drift dust-devils of sand around them.

The timing of the smoke would be critical—but the Germans had a device that served as a light agitation sensor. At least they had explained it as such. To Michael Rourke it sounded like a fancy term for a laser light detector.

He hoped.

He watched.

He could hear Maria Leuden breathing beside him. "Why haven't they fired yet?"

"It's not time yet—be patient. Patience is a virtue."

"But—"

"Just watch." Michael Rourke just watched. When the battle started, he would move, but not yet.

There was a flash of red stronger than before—he heard a whooshing sound and a dull thudding explosion.

There was a puff of heavy gray smoke, then suddenly clouds of the smoke billowed across the near face of the pyramid, and even with the naked eye, Michael Rourke could see the shafts of red laser light as they fired pencil thin lines across the expanse of desert and to the west.

"Have it!" The voice in his ear was Captain Hammerschmidt's.

Michael grabbed at Maria Leuden's right arm, half dragging her to her feet and after him, running, skidding, nearly falling along the windward side of the dune and down to the waiting SM-4, the Jeep-like vehicle's engine already running, Hammerschmidt's sergeant at the wheel. "Jump—quick!" He half lifted Maria Leuden into the rear seat, snatching the German assault rifle from her as he got one foot inside the front passenger seat and shouted to the sergeant, "Schnell!"

"Schnell!" the non-com laughed, stomping the accelerator pedal, the SM-4 spraying waves of sand behind its rear wheels as it slipped left, then started forward along the length of the dune. Hammerschmidt's voice in Michael's ear again. He was giving coordinates, Michael relaying them to Maria Leuden—a map flapped like a sail in her hands, in the slip-stream around the open SM-4.

"I've got it—a little over two kilometers—that way, sergeant!" And she gestured to the left of their line of travel.

"Yes, Fraulein Doctor," the man shouted back over the wind, cutting the wheel hard left, the SM-4's rear end fishtailing. Gunfire, mortar fire—the diversionary attack of Lieutenant Schmidt, fireballs rising in the distance near the Pyramid. When Michael Rourke had broached his plan, Maria Leuden had insisted on one thing—that the Great Pyramid in no way be harmed. With modern German surveying devices and x-raying techniques. Its mysteries might finally be yielded and to destroy it would have been doubly wrong. Michael had agreed.

He twisted in the seat, looking past her now at the billowing smoke behind them. Overhead now, German gunships crossed low over the dunes, missiles firing. But the Soviet force was too large for the attack to be more than a gesture now.

"To the left—about thirty degrees, sergeant."

"Yes, Fraulein Doctor!" The wheel cut again, the rear end slipping in the soft sand, digging in, skidding left then right, then the SM-4 accelerating.

Michael peeled away the keffiyeh, letting the wind catch at his hair, running his hands back through it, then stuffing the keffiyeh down inside his open shirt front as he slipped his arms from the jellaba.

He reached into the back seat—his M-16. He drew it up, across his lap, resisting the urge to cycle the action and chamber the top round off the thirty-round magazine already in place—in the bouncing and jostling SM-4, the chance of accidental discharge would be too great.

"About five degrees to your right, sergeant!"

"Yes, Fraulein Doctor," and the SM-4 skidded its

rear end left more than the front end turning right, the waves of sand around it again as the tires dug in, then the sensation of being compressed against the seat back.

On their right, he could see another of the SM-4s— it would be Hammerschmidt coming. To the west, he could see a line of the German mini-tanks his father had first told him of, that he had seen for himself the first time in the desert here the previous evening. They were purposely cutting oblique angles to the target area picked up by the German laser transits, to avoid leaving tracks that the desert winds might not quickly enough erase. And it was imperative to be out of range of Soviet gunships when they went off in pursuit of Lieutenant Schmidt's force.

The sound of explosions and gunfire was more distant now, the billowing smoke of the explosions, the occasional black and orange fireballs merely specks on the horizon. He glanced toward the SM-4's speedometer—approximately one hundred kilometers per hour—Michael mentally translated to miles—something between fifty-five and sixty was rough but good enough.

"We're almost there—it should be that dish-shaped valley to the east of us."

He glanced back to Maria Leuden—the German assault rifle was across her lap and in the sash around her waist was thrust the sheathed bayonet.

Michael Rourke mentally shrugged. Hammerschmidt was to take the lead—and Michael could see Hammerschmidt's SM-4 disappearing over the artificial horizon of a ridge of sand.

Already, the sergeant was cutting the wheel to follow.

Michael licked his lips, dry with the dusty wind. Karamatsov's forces would be airborne now, pursuing Milton Schmidt. But only a token force once Schmidt's withdrawal was apparent. Karamatsov would be making his way toward the site of whatever it was he had buried in the desert—and fast.

Michael hoped.

Chapter Ten

They had covered the SM-4s—four of them—with camouflage tarps to avoid detection from the air by ordinary observation. More sophisticated techniques involving electronic surveillance would spot the machines, but they were far enough off the probable line of travel to the coordinates located by the transits that the likelihood of more sophisticated sweeps of the area were remote. Karamatsov was noted for ruthlessness—not thoroughness.

The mini tanks were lost to him after the single sighting on the breakneck drive across the desert, but he knew their position would be five miles to the opposite side of the site, or approximately eight minutes travel time.

Three men were to be left behind with the SM-4s, men from Schmidt's detachment, Hammerschmidt and his sergeant and the five enlisted personnel gearing up as Michael dismounted the rise of sand, satisfied that Karamatsov was doing as anticipated. As he skidded down to the base, he called out in a low voice, "He's on the move—about five minutes travel time to the site. Those earth movers are slowing him up. Now here's what we'll do—as we planned it, Sergeant Dekker—you'll take three men and the Fraulein Doctor and cut to the south. Captain Ham-

91

merschmidt and the two remaining men and myself will cut to the north."

"We are ready here, Michael."

Michael Rourke nodded, his keffiyeh back in place against the strength of the sun, his M-16 caught up from beside the SM-4, where he had rested it. Mechanically, he checked the condition of readiness, working the bolt, setting the safety tumbler to safe.

Sergeant Dekker and each of his men had the German equivalent of LAWS rockets with them, each man with two of the weapons slung over each shoulder, their assault rifles in one hand or the other, their webbed gear festooned with grenades, fighting knives, communications devices and each man armed with a pistol as well.

Hammerschmidt's detachment was equipped much the same, Michael taking up a double brace of the rockets, slinging them as did the German soldiers.

He would learn Karamatsov's secret and perhaps have the opportunity to kill Karamatsov—Michael wondered somehow if learning the man's secret might somehow be a greater punishment.

But it wasn't that punishment Michael was most interested in . . .

John Thomas Rourke had erected one of the climatically controlled shelters while Natalia had kept the big man covered—the big man was called Char. And Jea—John Rourke's French was not good enough to make sense of the man's speech—had told Natalia that Char had pursued him because Char was the chief's son, and Char wanted the gun.

Char was unconscious still—John Rourke had assisted in that with a powerful sedative from his medical kit, compromising on the dosage between the man's apparent bulk and what it would take to put a normal-sized man out.

The tale that Jea told, related through Natalia—she had skinned away her coat now and despite a still apparent need for sleep seemed to have regained her strength—was a tale that to John Rourke seemed at once believable and horrible.

Among Jea's people there was no oral tradition, and no written tradition. Only Jea and his father and few others, most dead, could read at all or speak. But it seemed obvious, Rourke felt, that these people, like the exiles of Madison's home, the Place, were the result of being barely able to survive.

"Ask him a question for me," John Rourke began, lighting one of his thin, dark tobacco cigars, watching Jea's eyes, watching Jea's body language as the flame flickered from the battered Zippo. "Ask him where he got the rifle. I know he took it from Char's father, but where did Char's father get it?"

Rourke studied the glowing tip of the cigar as Natalia translated, going over it again and again, simplifying it into something Jea could finally understand at the end of the distillation process.

And then Jea began to speak—gestures of hands and arms and face accompanied each tortured syllable, Natalia interrupting frequently, trying to clarify meaning, then more gestures on Jea's part, more of the garbled French. Natalia nodded, patting Jea on the shoulder—Jea smiled, half the visible teeth in his mouth gone or broken.

"Our friend tells us that there are many tribes like his tribe, and that the ones in the black clothes and the helicopters—"

"How did he learn about helicopters, or are you—"

"Embroidering? No—I should have mentioned it. He spoke of a special book that his father used to

93

learn to read and speak with, and Jea has read it too. It was a comic book—Spiderman? Here—" And she opened the metal box Jea had set beside him.

John Rourke started to laugh—he glanced over toward Char, the huge one's body starting to stir slightly—but that was normal for the action of the sedative. Across Rourke's lap was the Python, to use as a club or to use to end Char's life, whichever, if either, was necessary.

"At any event, the ones in black, I assume forces from the Underground City, have slaughtered his people for years. The really healthy ones are taken away."

"Forced labor—or experimentation?"

"Probably both, but I'd tend to opt for the experimentation—there would be little that forced labor of Jea's training and background could provide a technologically advanced culture."

"Agreed—what else?"

"The gun," Natalia nodded, taking out one of the German non-carcinogenic cigarettes and Rourke lighting it for her. She had not actually returned to smoking—it was the third cigarette he had seen her smoke since leaving the Hekla community, and all things considered less a threat to health than his cigar. "Some of the ones in black came and one was killed with a rock. Char's father stole the rifle. The ones in black killed a considerable number of Jea's tribe and took only the younger of the women away. Jea's people are called the Blacks by the tribes to the south and west of here. Those tribes are naked most of the time, but Jea's people, because of the harsher climate here, wear the bark strip clothing, but the pigment in the bark darkens their skin—hence, the blacks."

"Artificial race—how marvelous," Rourke observed.

Natalia only nodded.

"Why did Jea steal the gun from Char—and run away? Are they inter-related, cause and effect or what?"

Again, John Rourke waited as Natalia labored over the translation, trying to find the simplest words and images to convey Rourke's thoughts to the trembling Jea. Natalia interrupted her work, digging in her pack, finding one of the thin, insulated blankets—similar to the Thermos Sportsmen's blankets of five centuries ago—and placing it around Jea's shoulders. Jea at first drew back, but characteristic of the blankets were the almost instant warmth they afforded. Jea stopped shaking, hugging the blanket around himself. Rourke doubted the origin of the tremors were body temperature. The bare fact of the man's survival here nearly naked under such unremitting cold indicated a hardiness of nature beyond that of conventional men.

Again, Natalia took up the translation.

John Rourke watched Char—the big man's stirring had not increased—the sedation was doing its work.

Finally, Natalia turned from Jea, her incredibly blue eyes seeming to mirror the light of the lantern set in the middle of the shelter floor. When Rourke had lit the lantern, Jea had to be restrained from flight.

"Char and his father have been becoming more and more brutal in their treatment of the rest of the tribe. Jea's father realized that there was something more, beyond their tribe, and that to improve his lot in life, Jea must find it. Jea took the gun to spare the rest of the tribe the potential of Char or Char's father using it. And as a means of defense since he was venturing out from the tribe and might encounter the ones in black. I gather Jea has no idea how to use the gun beyond the fact that it runs out of firepower after a time and the magazine needs to be replaced."

"He's a pretty sophisticated fellow, actually," Rourke observed.

"You are right," Natalia agreed. "We should be able to teach him his own language—French—or English without much difficulty."

"Ask him if he has any idea where the Underground City is, or where the tracks of the Russian APC were going in such a hurry."

Natalia nodded, then returned to interrogating Jea.

People—people who had reverted to primitivism, but John Rourke already held a certain admiration for them. Jea showed no evidence of cannibalism and there were sufficient plants here that it was conceivable that a tribe which spent the greatest part of daylight hours on the prowl for berries, nuts and other edible plant materials could subsist. The reason for Char's superior bulk seemed obvious as well—as the chief's son, he shared in the royal share of what the tribes scrounged for food. While others like Jea barely had enough food to survive. The healthier ones of the tribe would out of love or respect for age care for those who could not as easily fend for themselves as long as that were practical.

Rourke studied Jea—it seemed that the young man was in his early to middle thirties, but Rourke realized Jea was likely only in his teens. People would die quickly here.

A survival attempt that had gone wrong.

Natalia spoke. "It took a great deal of circumlocution. He knows the general location of the Underground City. And if the ones in black were moving quickly, he supposes they were going to the valley of the helicopters."

"Valley of the helicopters?"

"I asked him about it—and apparently it's some

96

sort of base away from the Underground City and large numbers of helicopters, tanks and equipment— at least I think he meant tanks—are gathering there. Some sort of staging area. But that doesn't make any sense, does it? I mean—wouldn't Vladmir be—ahh— well, from what Jea tells me, the Underground City is reasonably close. Within a day's travel. I doubt Jea would run it—he doesn't look to have the stamina. But we can't be talking more than twenty miles."

John Rourke studied the tip of his cigar.

"We have to see this place Jea talks about. As soon as we can. If it's a staging area, we have to find out for what. We can leave here in a little while, once I'm certain Char's sedative is wearing off properly. Once he's starting to revive. We can't leave the man to freeze to death and it would be like a calling card to leave the shelter here. You get some sleep—tell Jea to do the same. I'll stand watch over our friend. You're sure Jea isn't just bullshitting because we sound interested?"

"I'm sure."

John Rourke only nodded—he'd gone for longer periods without sleep.

Char was still stirring on the floor of the shelter.

Chapter Eleven

Michael Rourke edged forward, the dunes having given way to ruins that he judged were millenia old, a temple-like structure with cracking columns thrusting skyward only to be broken, jagged, crumbling, their debris littering the sandswept stones of the flooring beneath his feet.

He worked his way ahead a column at a time, Hammerschmidt in the lead on the opposite side of the ancient walkway, one of Hammerschmidt's enlisted men dogging Hammerschmidt a column behind, the other doing the same behind Michael.

Michael crossed to the next column, a hot wind playing with the edges of the keffiyeh he wore, the twin Beretta 92SB-F 9mm military pistols in his fists, the safeties swung up into the fire position.

He felt the muscles at the corners of his eyes tighten as he peered from beyond the column.

Karamatsov's perimeter security had been arranged oddly and the only means of penetrating the site of the dig—the only means which had immediately presented itself at least—was through the temple corridor. Guards were stationed at the far end, the Animov-60 assault rifles held leisurely enough, but at the ready all the same. Four guards—it translated to one each for Michael, Hammerschmidt, and the two enlisted men, Hammerschmidt's commandos.

But Michael looked beyond them now—beyond the guards to the excavation site, no careful archeological dig here. Earth movers gulping huge amounts of sand, then disgorging the sand into heaps between the temple from which Michael observed and the pit they dug itself.

Perhaps a supply of nuclear weapons. Perhaps something worse. But it might be the chance to kill Karamatsov and at the very least to confound the "Hero Marshal's" plans. He'd thought at times since the death of his wife what he would say to his father, if his father in fact still did not know, as was likely the case. My wife is dead—your grandchild will never be born. He had thought of saying it that way, of saying it dozens of other ways. But he wanted, for his own sanity and the sanity of his father, to say, but I killed Karamatsov.

A half dozen columns remaining separated Michael and Hammerschmidt across from him from the four guards at the end of the temple walkway. The guards stood in the shade, their black uniforms, battle dress utilities, looking insufferably hot here.

Michael glanced across the aisle to Hammerschmidt, Hammerschmidt nodding as Michael worked down the ambidexterous safeties of his pistols, then one at a time holstered them beneath his arms and the folds of the jellaba.

As his right hand re-emerged, he held the Life Support System II knife, ready. Another glance at Hammerschmidt and Michael stepped into the walkway, edging quickly forward now, but careful of his footing lest he twist an ankle on the rough surfaced walkway, lest he dislodge a chunk of paving and make a betraying noise.

From the corner of his left eye he could see Hammerschmidt moving similarly forward, one of the German bayonets in his left fist, a fighting knife of smaller proportions than the knife Michael held, clenched tight in Hammerschmidt's other hand.

He could hear the telltale scratching sounds of shifting sand behind him—the enlisted man who was his shadow.

Four against four—but silently.

Michael moved ahead, taking long strided steps, making certain of the footing with each movement.

He had to refocus his thoughts—he was thinking of the man who would be his target and who would somehow betray him, he knew. Why, he did not know.

He thought of Madison—and his stomach tightened, his throat tightened—hatred for these men who killed like blunt instruments, who assaulted the innocent.

He kept edging forward, seeing now as the commando who was his shadow fell in beside him, to his left, the commando with Hammerschmidt to that man's left, Hammerschmidt at the far end. They had discussed it briefly, planning it like a ballet.

Choreography.

The choreography called for all four to strike the four guards at the end of the temple at once. If one of the guards turned around, got off a shot—Michael kept moving, the knife kept at chest level lest somehow the movement, the rustle of the fabric of his jellaba alert the guards.

Michael Rourke kept moving. Six feet to go and Michael nodded, raising the knife. He focused his concentration on the knife rather than the man—a design unchanged in five centuries, a faithful duplicate of the handmade original. He wondered if his father knew Jack Crain. A man who made a knife like this sounded like the kind of man his father would have counted a friend.

Three feet—one long step.

Michael took it, his left hand like a claw, swinging across the body plane of the guard on the far right, over the mouth, the knife raking hard across the throat and slitting the windpipe. On the backswing, Michael twisted the blade downward, stabbing into the chest in the general area of the heart. The man was already dead as Michael dragged him into the deeper shade of the temple.

For the first time, he glanced to his left—Hammerschmidt and his two enlisted men had claimed their targets as well.

Michael wiped the blade of his knife clean against the Soviet guard's black BDU blouse and resheathed it, snapping the Beretta pistols from the leather.

He approached the edge of the temple where the guards had stood, the two enlisted men propping up the guards against the temple columns near to where they had originally stood, using long pieces of rigid steel cable coils slipped down the rear of the dead men's uniforms. From a distance he supposed the appearance that the dead men stood under their own power would be satisfactory.

He dismissed the idea, scanning the approximate quarter mile of desert which separated him from the dig site. It was imperative to know exactly when the Russians had freed whatever they searched for from the sands.

He could hear the hiss of the rope snaking upward and he glanced behind him—the pneumatic powered rapelling rope launcher had fired. There was a telltale click and his eyes instantly returned to the desert. There was no sign the sound had been heard. He could see Karamatsov, strutting near the equipment that was doing the digging—near but not too near.

Others officers with Karamatsov, as though guarding him, shielding him. Had he his father's Steyr-Mannlicher SSG, he could have killed Karamatsov if he timed it right for movement. Had he his father's eye, he could have taken Karamatsov with one of the iron sighted German assault rifles. But he had neither the sniper rifle nor his father's peculiar gift. He considered himself as good as his father with a handgun, albeit not as experienced—he doubted anyone was quite as good a rifleman. His father seemed to be able to turn off impatience, turn off anger, focus total concentration to the task. Michael strove for this, but had not yet attained it. He smiled at the thought—but being a Rourke, he had the confidence to be certain that some day he would.

Sand, the sound of bits of rock showering down—he looked back into the temple—one of the two enlisted men was already rapelling along the height of the column, field binoculars suspended in air space behind his back, the second enlisted man holding the first man's rifle.

Hammerschmidt edged toward Michael. "So far, so good, I believe the expression is."

"Yes—so far so good."

"Perhaps then you shall have your revenge today. Or Karamatsov's secret."

"Or both," Michael grinned. "But you're probably right—one or the other, and the secret is probably the more important."

"You are a good man to work beside, Herr Rourke."

"Michael."

"Otto," Hammerschmidt nodded.

"Otto," Michael repeated.

Hammerschmidt and Michael Rourke turned as one—the sound of falling bits of rock had stopped.

Michael shielded his eyes from the sun which was bright above them beyond the shadows of the columns—the enlisted man was in place, Hammerschmidt holding the listening piece of his radio to his ear. "The digging is nearly complete, my corporal thinks—he is an intelligent man and has keen powers of observation. He is likely correct."

"Any idea—"

"Wait—he tells me that there is a large cylinder, of the type used for the underground storage of gasoline. It seems to be of stainless steel or titanium—it is completely untarnished and appears unscratched from the abrasiveness of the sand—it is almost mirror bright. They are moving in a helicopter with a crane—there to the west."

Michael took his own binoculars and raised them, pushing the button for automatic focusing—a shape like a huge skeletal insect was coming off the horizon.

The second enlisted man broke Michael's concentration. "Herr Captain—"

Michael looked to the man as did Hammerschmidt. The young private held a radio set headset to his ear, the radio itself strapped to his back. "Herr Captain—I have been monitoring the Soviet transmissions as you requested. Marshal Karamatsov himself is directing the recovery operation. He is cautioning the crew of the helicopter that utmost care must be taken. He is ordering all his personnel to fall back except those in the final recovery detail. I heard a reference, Herr Captain, to protective clothing."

"Gas?" Hammerschmidt mused aloud, it seemed.

"Maybe—maybe worse," Michael nodded, seeing Karamatsov and his people fall back at a rapid jog toward their vehicles, men in protective clothing—the purpose not certain—rushing toward the cannister.

"We have no protective clothing. I advise we withdraw to a safer distance. We should perhaps rethink attempting to steal Marshal Karamatsov's prize—you would agree?"

"If we don't know what we're handling—wait—" And Michael shifted the binoculars quickly, focusing on a dark shape beneath the helicopter, farther away on the horizon. It was a truck, a cloud of dust behind it, almost surrounding it, but a truck of immense proportions. "Take a look at that," Michael whispered.

"Himmel—that is huge. For the cannister?"

"Get your man up top to take a look." And Michael heard Hammerschmidt speaking in German into the transceiver. "Well?"

"He estimates the size as one hundred meters in length—it appears to have eight axles and triple tires on each side of each axle."

"A truck specially built to haul that thing he dug up—whatever it is."

"Wait—there is more, Michael." Michael Rourke watched Hammerschmidt's blue eyes as they focused into pinpoints of light. "He cannot be certain, but the suspension seems to be massive."

"Do they have an aircraft that could haul that tank—and the truck?"

"It would seem possible. Lieutenant Schmidt told me that their airfield is substantially larger than he would have thought necessary."

"What is it and where are they taking it—shit!" Michael snarled.

"There is a way to find out, I think. My man up above—he says there are men hanging to the sides of the truck, on catwalks—two men on each side. They wear protective clothing—it includes some type of headgear that covers the face."

Michael Rourke licked his lips.

104

"We might wind up following it back to Russia."

"The Underground City—then all the better, hum, Michael?"

Michael Rourke focused on the truck—he could see the men now too. The two on the truck's right side looked the right size for himself and Hammerschmidt.

"Why not," Michael almost whispered. In the final analysis with Madison and the baby gone, he had little to lose.

Chapter Twelve

Jea knew the ground here like an animal would know a trail through the woods, Rourke observed, the boy moving effortlessly along the rocky escarpment, climbing goat-like—but Jea would not know what a goat was, or an animal. The only animals he would know of were people. There was more animalistic behavior in some of the people the boy knew anyway than in anything wild, Rourke thought.

Rourke had discussed with Natalia the likelihood that the names Jea had provided—Jea's own, the bullying barrel-chested Char—that they were corruptions of actual names passed down through the years since Jea and the people like him were forced to survive upon the surface. That it was a survival experiment which had gone wrong was obvious, and John Rourke looked forward to examining Jea and others of his people. It was evident that they had returned to the surface when background radiation was still hot enough to affect them. The leathery-looking skin, the odd color of Jea's eyes—human but not usual. Char, too, had those same eyes.

As they moved, Rourke's own eyes assessed the young man—a slightly abnormal flare to the ears, again something shared with the bear-like Char. The cheekbones were large beyond normal and the nostrils widely flared.

Yet all the human qualities seemed to be there—

kinship, aggression, fear, the desire to know perhaps most importantly there.

Jea raised both hands, as though surrendering to some unseen enemy, but Rourke judged it a gesture signalling a halt.

Natalia approached closer to the young man and began to converse with him. Rourke passed them both, dropping into a crouch, cautiously going along the tongue of rock which extended ahead of them, his eyes scanning side to side for evidence that indeed they had reached the mysterious Soviet staging area.

He stopped short, drawing back.

He heard Natalia's barely whispered words behind him. "Jea tells me we have arrived."

"He's a master of understatement—look—and keep Jea back."

A few murmurs from Natalia, then Rourke dropped to a prone position, starting ahead through the snow along the tongue of rock, Natalia doing the same beside him.

It was a perfect vantage point. Soviet tanks of the type seen in the battle in Argentina, ranked six abreast and stretching nearly as far as the eye could see. Helicopter gunships. APCs like the one they had followed—and troops everywhere encamped in tents like those he and Natalia had seen earlier when the Soviet patrol they had followed had encamped for the night. Quonset huts made up the more permanent dwellings of the encampment.

It was an army more massive than Rourke had seen since that time so long ago that he had viewed Soviet tanks crossing the Khyber Pass, the thing that had begun it all, changed his life, the lives of the people he loved, the lives of all humanity irreparably.

John Rourke doubted the Germans could field such a force while still retaining even nominal security at their Complex in Argentina.

The lines of supply would be difficult, almost impossible, unless some lightning strike could take the Russians out.

"John—over there—I saw something!"

John Rourke glanced to Natalia, then across the gulf which separated the tongue of rock from the rock wall opposite them. He judged the distance as a thousand yards or better. But he saw movement under the gray sun. "Down—tell Jea!"

Natalia said something that wasn't quite French, the snow and rock beside them spraying up.

"A sniper!"

Rourke pushed Natalia flat into the snow, shrugging the SSG off his shoulder, shifting it forward, popping away the scope covers, checking the scope setting—three power—as he cheeked to the green synthetic stock. There was no sound—but he felt the snow spray cold against his cheek. "A silencer?"

"Gotta be a closed breech weapon—a single shot—that's why it's taking him so long to reload. Get Jea down and out of here—back the way we came—I'll be with you." Rourke gradually started increasing magnification, trying to acquire the sniper. "Go on."

"No—he'll—"

"He'll have a radio—but he won't have had time to use it yet maybe. There'll be Soviet troops up here fast one way or the other. But they won't pinpoint us a hundred percent until I open up. Get outa here—"

"But a thousand meters or better, John—"

"Shouldn't be too bad a shot with this—I got him—run for it," and Rourke blocked Natalia Anastasia Tiemerovna from his consciousness now, moving the scope only slightly so at full magnification he wouldn't lose the Soviet sniper. There wasn't a clear shot yet. The man would have to profile himself just a little bit more on the wall of rock to get into a perfect shooting position.

He saw movement, what could only be a right shoulder and a dark shape taped or painted with irregular white patterns being brought to the shoulder.

The head—John Rourke saw the head.

His right hand worked the bolt of the SSG effortlessly, settling the bolt closed, one of the .308 Boat-tails chambered. His right first finger snapped off the rearmost of the double triggers, setting the first for a pull that was barely a nudge.

The sniper's head.

The gun was firing—John Rourke couldn't move lest he would lose the shot.

His right first finger brushed against the forward trigger, the Steyr's crack like a thunderbolt in the cold, rarefied air, the otherwise total stillness. The snow pelted against the exposed skin of his left cheek—he realized he had removed the toque without thinking.

The rifle butt punched against his shoulder.

The sniper's body seemed frozen for an instant, Rourke settling the scope again, the man's eyes lost in distance, but something about the set of the bone structure beneath the white toque which covered the man's face—and then redness where the white had been a fraction of a second earlier, the body lurching forward, rolling, slipping, billowing clouds of snow giving way around it—and it was gone, sailing downward in the air.

Rourke rolled onto his back—he breathed.

To his feet, despite the snowshoes, running—already he could hear the sounds of engines starting in the valley below.

Chapter Thirteen

It wasn't a job for a knife, Hammerschmidt had said and Michael Rourke had agreed.

The wire commando saw would make a perfect garrote, but would cut through fabric and flesh and achieve the same negative result as a knife.

Michael Rourke had early on developed a fondness for history—and he showed Otto Hammerschmidt how to utilize the material of the keffiyehs they both wore as a scarf with a thugee knot.

The monstrously large truck had stopped, the cargo helicopter's crane lifting the massive and gleaming cylinder from the trench in the sand. All eyes in the area of the excavation site seemed to be turned skyward. Michael broke from the cover of the nearer of the sand mounds built by the earth moving equipment, the mound nearer the partially destroyed temple where they had hidden.

He ran, a long strided, low, loping run, stripped of his gear save for the double shoulder rig and the spare magazines for the Berettas and his fighting knife, the improvised thugee scarf wound in both his tight-clenched fists, the two men on the truck's catwalk nearest him seemingly enrapt with the precarious swinging of the massive cylinder at the end of the helicopter's crane nearly directly overhead now.

It was eight feet to the catwalk from the desert floor.

Michael glanced left—Hammerschmidt was about a half stride behind him.

Michael jumped, his hands going out, hurtling his weight across the catwalk, nearly knocking the decontamination suited man into the cylindrically shaped basin in the truck bed—the truck was designed specifically for the cylinder, Michael realized. Michael looped the scarf about the man's throat as the man started to turn. But Michael turned first, a full one hundred eighty degrees—his father had taught him the technique. The knot should have crushed the man's Adam's Apple—and as Michael flipped the man backward over his left shoulder and down from the catwalk to the sand, he heard a loud snapping sound, almost as loud as a light caliber pistol shot like a .22—the neck breaking at least, perhaps the back.

But the noise of the cargo chopper overhead would have masked the sound, Michael told himself. There was a blur of silver—the second man in decontamination gear. Michael jumped to the sand, onto the back of the first man, hammering his right fist against the neck that logic already told him was broken, but making sure. The body didn't move.

Left. Right. Michael's eyes scanned the area around them, but there was no alarm. Overhead, if the helicopter's cable snapped, the truck would be crushed and so would he and Hammerschmidt. Already, Michael's hands were finding the fasteners for the decontamination suit, opening it—the man's eyes beneath the masked headgear were open wide in a mixture of death and astonishment.

Michael Rourke had the headgear free, the decontamination suit a coverall fitted with a backpack with double cylinders—Michael presumed some sort of oxygen mixture. Whatever was in the cannister—he couldn't conjecture beyond the fact that it was dangerous.

He had the suit nearly stripped away now, praying silently that it would fit, not only well enough to appear normal, but be large enough to conceal the few weapons he had brought.

He had the man out of the suit now—loose fitting, thin black coveralls were beneath it. He left these—no time anyway. He started into the decontamination suit. There was no need to remove his own boots—the dead man's boots were similar and the decontamination suit's trouser legs were closed at the bottom to cover footgear. The four pack of Beretta magazines, like the Sparks Six-Pack his father carried for his Detonics pistols. It would have bulged too much, Michael had realized. He had stripped the magazines from it, leaving the four pack with his pistol belt and the rest of the gear. Two twenty-round magazines he had added from his backpack. He pulled into the upper portion of the suit, the breathing unit one piece with the suit, apparently serving a cooling function as well, despite the suit's reflective surface.

It covered the double shoulder rig—adequately, not perfectly. But good enough, he hoped. He left the headgear off for a moment longer. He had stuffed his knife, sheath and all into the waistband of his Levis and he drew it out now, using the bootlace-like tie down on the belt loop to secure it around his left calf beneath the suit. He square knotted it in place, then knotted over again just to be safe—he remembered his father's words—"Plan ahead." He sealed the suit legs along the inseams of the thighs, then sealed the front of the suit at the top, forcing the headgear down over his face.

He glanced to Hammerschmidt—the German captain was nearly suited up.

Michael left his hands out of the suit's attached gloves—with his bare hands now, he started plowing sand, digging as shallow a grave as necessary to cover the body from casual view.

Overhead, the cylinder was lowering into position—he would be expected on the catwalk. Soon all eyes would be on the truck—at any moment the missing men would be discovered. He rolled the body into the sand, automatically thumbing closed the eyelids. A human being was still a human being. He shoved and pushed sand over the body.

"Good enough," Michael Rourke hissed, jumping to his feet, running to the catwalk, no time to climb the ladder-like steps at the side. He jumped—he nearly lost his balance, nearly falling into the space made to nest the cylinder.

But he didn't fall.

Slipping his hands into his suit's gloves, he saw Hammerschmidt, behind him.

The cylinder was lowering, the men on the opposite side of the catwalk taking long handled, hooked objects like massive boat hooks—he had seen these in films—and reaching upward and outward to the cylinder.

Michael took up one of the hooks from the rack beside the catwalk and did the same—they were guiding the cylinder into its berth.

Behind him, he heard a voice he had heard once before—it spoke in Russian and he nodded slightly as if in response.

The voice was that of Vladmir Karamatsov, close enough to kill.

"Not yet," Michael almost verbalized. He had his hook to the cylinder—so did Hammerschmidt.

Michael stole a glance behind him—Karamatsov, in

decontamination gear, was moving away.

The cylinder was nearly in place. There was more shouting in Russian, but a different voice now. Michael watched for Hammerschmidt to react from the corner of his left eye, his peripheral vision cut by the suit's face mask. Hammerschmidt spoke Russian.

There was a resounding clunking sound and the cable slackened—the cylinder was down and a cheer went up in the distance from the black suited men and nearby from those few like him in decontamination gear.

Michael turned to Hammerschmidt as though elated—he whispered, "We're in deep shit."

Hammerschmidt didn't answer.

Chapter Fourteen

John Rourke lost his balance, regained it and jumped, keeping the Steyr, the scope covers back in place, high, protecting it against impact as he hit the snow, rolled, skidded and stopped. The M-16 across his back impacted his spine. "Shit," he snarled.

Ahead, he could see the snowshoe tracks of Natalia, the bark shoe prints of Jea.

To his feet—he started running again, more of the mechanical noises behind him now—soon helicopters would be airborne. Soon.

He looked behind him—nothing.

He ran, the loping, awkward run that snowshoes imposed, like a bizarre shuffle.

His mind raced faster than his legs. Why would Karamatsov—"Damn," he hissed. There was only one reason he could fathom, and it fit Karamatsov's personality, fit the whole idea of the construction of the Womb which Karamatsov had initiated and Rozhdestvensky, Karamatsov's successor in KGB when it had been thought Vladmir Karamatsov was dead, had continued.

Rourke quickened his pace. A mechanical noise, suddenly loud, growling almost directly behind him.

He looked back—an armored snow tractor, but the armor would be light to prevent its getting bogged down in drifts.

He scanned to right and left—rocks to the left. He veered off at an oblique angle, starting for them, the snow tractor almost on top of him, machinegun fire from a turret atop the vehicle, the snow rising up in waves around him. But there was no sense shooting back.

The rocks—less than fifty yards remained.

John Rourke reached to his right exterior pocket. He had planned ahead.

One of the German high explosive grenades from his backpack.

He detested the habit, but had only one free hand, baring his teeth and biting down hard on the ring for the pin, ripping it free, his left fist holding the rifle, his right fist holding the grenade's spoon tight against the body. He jumped and wheeled, lobbing the grenade more like a bowling ball than a baseball which would have better matched its size.

The left tread of the snow tractor started to veer right.

The grenade—Rourke hurtled himself to the snow, the concussion dislodging mounds of snow along the rock face near him, his body instantly showered with it, his ears ringing a little as he pushed himself to his feet.

The snow tractor was overturned.

He slung the SSG across his back, no time to grab for the M-16, his left hand working the fasteners at the front of his parka, his right hand to his mouth, biting away the overglove he had replaced after firing the Steyr counter-sniper rifle. His right hand flashed under his jacket to the little Detonics .45 under his left armpit, his left hand between his knees, tearing away the other glove. As the little stainless .45 broke from the leather, he shifted the pistol into his left hand, his right fist popping the closure for the flap holster at his right hip, finding the butt of the Python where subconscious memory told him it almost always was.

He had it, his left thumb flicking back the .45's hammer, his right fist closing on the Pachmayr gripped butt of the Metalifed and Mag-Na-Ported Python as it cleared leather.

From the nearly inverted top hatch of the snow tractor—Rourke shuffled left, getting clear for the shots. A man—an Animov-60 assault rifle in both fists—Rourke made the little Detonics do a double tap, the man's body collapsing, half hanging out of the turret, then suddenly being thrust clear. Rourke threw himself to the snow as assault rifle fire broke the air, bullets chewed into the snow and rocks beside him.

He rolled onto his back, firing the Python overhead toward the turret, by feel only, the sights useless to him this way—he double actioned the Colt .357 twice, the assault rifle still now.

To his stomach, the revolver and the self-loader thrust ahead of him. To his feet. Rourke glanced to right and left, then advanced on the snow tractor. There was no more movement and he judged it likely there had only been two men. But he had grenades to waste. He shifted his left thumb behind the Detonics mini-gun's tang and upped the safety, then shoved the pistol under his right armpit.

The grenade from his left pocket.

He did the thing with his teeth again—he'd known men to break teeth doing it and had no desire to join their ranks. But he pulled the pin, spat the ring and pin into the snow and tossed the grenade through the hatch, grabbing his pistol, running a few yards and throwing himself down as the concussion came again, but not so loudly, the shell of the snow tractor muffling it.

Onto his back, chunks of burning debris raining down, much of the undercarriage of the snow tractor blown outward in jagged, teeth-like shapes.

He pushed himself up to his feet, stuffing the little Detonics .45 into his left outside pocket.

Rourke's eyes scanned the ground—he started back toward his gloves. Mentally, he noted to check the Steyr for damage from the rolls he'd taken with it on his back. But it was a sturdy weapon. If anything had sustained trauma, it would be the scope. He could shoot the SSG nearly as well with the iron sights anyway.

Both gloves in his left hand, he started back toward his original path.

The choppers would be coming very quickly now and he still had to catch up with Natalia and Jea. He kept the Python, four rounds still in the cylinder, tight in his right fist as he moved ahead . . .

Maria sat with her knees tight together, the jellaba folded over her legs, her hands folded in her lap despite the jostling of the SM-4 across the desert.

The attack had been cancelled—Captain Hammerschmidt had given specific orders to Sergeant Dekker and she didn't know anything specific about them—but the attack was cancelled and Michael Rourke and Otto Hammerschmidt had vanished, promising further radio contact.

Then there had been the two remaining elements of Hammerschmidt's Commando force—she had sucked in her breath so loudly that it had sounded like a scream, she knew.

Michael Rourke and Otto Hammerschmidt had

substituted themselves for two of the guards on the massive truck which had taken the cannister away across the desert.

Dekker—the older man had taken her aside. Had it shown that much, she wondered?

"Fraulein Doctor—doubtlessly the Herr Captain will activate the tracking device in his radio and we will know where they are. This will lead us perhaps to the Soviet Underground City. The Herr Captain—and the young Herr Rourke, too, I think—they are good soldiers, Fraulein."

She had leaned her head against his chest and murmured thanks to him, then climbed aboard the SM-4 again.

And she sat there now, letting her body sway with the rhythm of the vehicle.

She realized that she was falling in love with someone who couldn't return her love. And if time were, as it was put in books, to heal his wounds, would there be time enough?

She pushed the coarse wool shawl down from her head, running her splayed fingers back through her hair, letting the desert wind catch it.

She had removed her glasses and she closed her eyes now, telling herself that the stinging felt in her eyes was the stinging of the wind only.

Chapter Fifteen

There had been more men in decontamination suits waiting at the desert airfield and the truck had been driven directly up the ramp of the huge airlifter and the hatchway sealed, Michael feeling it in the pit of his stomach as the aircraft had left the ground— feeling the sensation of movement, feeling the sensation of being close to death.

Hammerschmidt had whispered as Michael and the German commando leader had drifted into seats on long benches which flanked the truck on either side, that though his Russian was adequate, he assumed his accent to be terrible, and five hundred years out of date.

This hadn't built Michael's confidence.

Michael Rourke kept his arms by his sides, to cover the telltale bulgers of his pistols beneath the decontamination suit.

When he thought no one was looking, he would glance at his Rolex—not too often but often enough to figure the duration of the trip.

His mind was assessing possibilities. There were sixteen other men—some of them could have been women but it was hard to tell with the decontamination suits—aboard the craft, plus the aircrew in the sealed compartment forward, perhaps some security personnel as well.

In theory at least, it was possible to kill all the others in the decontamination suits without reloading his pistols, giving two shots each. In theory, Hammerschmidt's training would enable him to land the massive aircraft. But where?

And in theory, he had no theory as to the contents of the cannister. The decontamination suits could have been safety precaution alone, or potential necessity.

His father had told him once, "Don't make a plan and then throw yourself into it just because you have nothing else to do. The key to a successful plan—in life, in combat, in a survival situation, even in a fistfight—the key is knowledge of the situation, as full and complete knowledge as you can ascertain. And use this knowledge to formulate your plan, then act upon it. In the meantime, hang back and keep out of range or out of trouble or whatever. Patience Michael—it's more than a virtue. It's a necessity."

It was pleasantly comfortable inside the decontamination suit—but he was still perspiring.

One of the men beside him began to talk to him, the voice muffled sounding through the headgear.

Michael closed his eyes for an instant—and he made a mental note that if he got out of this alive, he'd get Natalia to work more with him on vernacular Russian . . .

Annie Rubenstein started at the helicopter two hundred yards from the tent through the plastic window, a snowstorm lazily sweeping the German forward base in what had been Finland. But the snowstorm's ferocity was not nearly so intense that they could not have gone on, would have been grounded by it.

But there was no way to find her father and Natalia and Captain Hartman. They had been inserted deep into Soviet territory and the helicopters or whatever had brought them had left, awaiting recall by radio and there was no radio transmission. There was no way to locate them.

"Shit," she hissed, thrusting her hands into the pockets of her skirt and turning back to face the interior of the tent, to face her husband.

Paul played poker for cartridges with the German pilot who had brought them here and the lieutenant who oversaw the forward base, the other half dozen personnel and the other pilots sleeping through the storm, only a radio officer and the perimeter guards otherwise awake.

She looked back through the tent window to the helicopters and fighter planes further out from the tent. She could see the radar masts when the snow cleared for an instant, see the radar dishes searching the skies. The skies—more rare to see—were gray.

They had arrived and been informed that there was still no word from Hartman and that they would have to wait here.

Paul had changed out of his arctic gear and she had changed out of the pants she had worn beneath hers. Paul had laughed at her seeing her in pants—and she realized it was the first time he had ever seen her in pants, she wore them so infrequently.

Annie began to move about the tent. The living quarters given over to herself and her husband were at the far end of the circus-sized tent. She debated going there, resting—but she couldn't rest.

It was impossible to consider the tent as a conventional structure. It was a seemingly one piece and totally sealed structure with an airlock-like entryway, completely climate controlled. She was almost too warm with the sweater she had thrown across her shoulders.

She had played poker for a while and been winning—when Paul had realized why he had whispered to her, "You shouldn't do that."

"I can't help it—I'm nervous," she had responded, folding her hand and getting up to go stare out the window. She had noticed that at times of heightened stress her peculiar mental abilities were also heightened. Without trying—in fact trying consciously not to—she had been reading everyone's hand at the table. She had won almost five hundred rounds of the German caseless assault rifle ammunition.

The ammunition was only a means of keeping score—but she supposed it was cheating anyway.

No—she couldn't go back to the poker game.

She took a folding camp chair on the far wall of the tent, away from the poker game, her bag beside the chair from when she had first left their living quarters. She opened the bag, taking out her embroidery, checking the tightness of the hoop, smoothing the material within the circumference of the hoop and examining the design. It was based on one of her mother's paintings that had been used to illustrate the childrens books her mother had written before the Night of The War. A tiger, his eyes gleaming as he sat very quietly and protective beside a lop eared rabbit. The rabbit almost vanished between his massive front paws.

She had dozed on the helicopter flight from Iceland to here—and she had dreamed, this time of Michael. She had asked the radio officer if Michael could be contacted, but again told that strict radio silence was the safest course of action.

The interior of the air-lock like doorway from the

outside opened, the radio officer entered the room.

Paul stood, throwing his cards face down on the camp table.

The radio officer—who spoke excellent English—announced, "We have just had a short radio message in code from our troops in Egypt, Frau Rubenstein, Herr Rubenstein. It appears the young Herr Rourke and Captain Hammerschmidt have hidden themselves among a Soviet unit and are at this moment somewhere en route to the Soviet Underground City."

Annie dropped the embroidery hoop to her lap, both her hands going to her mouth.

In the dream, Michael and Karamatsov had been so close they could almost touch—and somehow Michael had been in terrible danger.

She began to cry and after a moment noticed that Paul knelt beside her, his arms around her and she leaned her head then, against his shoulder . . .

Vladmir Karamatsov paced the fuselage of his private jet, eyeing Nicolai Antonovich's decoded message.

Ivan Krakovski cleared his throat.

Karamatsov looked at him, stopping his pacing. "You wish to know the contents of your rival's message."

"Comrade Marshal—I—"

"Never considered him a rival for your colonelcy? He is a better officer, a better leader, a more sensitive person than you. Which is why he is not your rival, why he is holding a small force in waiting to attack the Eden Project and why you are here with me. For my purpose, you are the better man. And my purposes are all that concern me, Ivan." It was the first time he had ever called Krakovski by anything other than his last name or his rank and he watched Krakovski's face—the significance was not lost on the junior officer.

"Comrade Marshal—I—" and Krakovski stood.

Krakovski was very military, his uniform footgear polished to mirror brightness, the creases in his BDU trousers and jacket seemingly razor sharp. Karamatsov found himself smiling—no doubt the bore of his pistol was spotless as well.

"Sit down, my friend—and I shall tell you many things."

Krakovski almost sagged into his seat.

Karamatsov peered out the window—there was open ocean beneath the aircraft now, wisps of white cloud beneath them as well. He turned his eyes—squinting—away from the sunlight and to the message in his hands. "Antonovitch tells us that the Eden Project base has been reinforced by several hundred German troops, German troops with tanks and other heavy equipment and large numbers of helicopter gunships. I find all of this excellent. I have succeeded in dividing my enemy's forces—Iceland, Georgia, Argentina, and as we learned during that useless little attack they made at the site of the Great Pyramid, in Egypt as well. Meanwhile, the Politburo believes our troops are equally divided—massing for attack on the new German base outside Mt. Hekla in Iceland, massing for attack against the German headquarters in Argentina. In reality, Antonovitch's small force in Georgia and his few spies outside the German Argentinian headquarters represent the smallest fragment of my army. Our purpose in Egypt has been achieved—" and Karamatsov stared out the window again, lowering his frame to see at level with the mighty cargo lifter which carried the precious cargo he had invaded Egypt to obtain. Surrounding the cargo craft and his own jet were other cargo lifters, helicopter gunships, tanks and other equipment and personnel inside them. "So—we no longer have forces in Egypt. At last report, our staging base outside the Underground City had not yet been detected. Were it to be detected even at this moment, it would be too late. The power is now mine, and I shall need a man who is possessed of as little scruple as am I to assist me in my endeavors. That, Ivan Vassilivich Krakovski, is why you are with me now. See that you stay with me and your future will be assured. Even I cannot rule an entire planet unaided."

"Comrade Marshal—the cannister extracted from the sand there beside the temple—"

"The world five centuries ago was a place, Ivan—a place you cannot imagine—at least to me. Everywhere, there were the seeds of revolution. The leadership of the Party was falling into the decadence they themselves decried, and yet—yet—the millions flocked to Communism, Ivan. And I realized that through Communism, I could achieve greater ends than any man had achieved before. Through my agents, carefully structuring the intelligence data presented to the Kremlin leadership, I was able to advance the cause of war, bring World War III closer, closer. And then it came—my dream. My opportunity, Ivan. And I prepared for every eventuality. With my planning for the Womb which Rozhdestvenskiy let slip through his fingers, with my involvement with the Underground City. And with the cannister which so intrigues you. Tell me—what do you think it contains?"

Karamatsov turned away from the window—he could see only dark spots in his eyes until he squinted, having stared so long into the light. But now he could see Ivan Krakovski.

"I—nerve gas, Comrade Marshal—perhaps that."

Vladmir Karamatsov shook his head, allowed himself to smile.

"More deadly. And I shall use it to make myself the master—of all that—" and he gestured expansively toward what lay beyond the windows of his private aircraft. It was the world.

Chapter Sixteen

They had hidden under rock and overhangs—Jea knew the territory well. And after many hours, Natalia sleeping fitfully, Rourke still not allowing himself the luxury, the skies had cleared of helicopter gunships and again they had pressed on through the snow, the sun declining rapidly now.

Hartman would have to be notified—but first to locate the Underground City, the intelligence report complete then.

He remembered the old days, not just before the Night of The War, but before he had decided that his life's work would be survival training and weapons training, the days after he had given up on a career in medicine and joined the Central Intelligence Agency.

It was there that he had first met Natalia—in a manner of speaking.

It was there that he had learned that intelligence gathering required intuitive knowledge tempered with logic and an understanding of the immediate situation—rather than bare facts alone which could be misleading out of context.

But with the coordinates of the Underground City and the coordinates of the staging area, Hartman would have all the data needed.

What to do with it was another question. Conventional saturation bombing was a possibility, a protracted ground war with the Soviet force on their own ground almost predestined for failure.

Once they reached Jea's approximate location of the Underground City, once Rourke had gathered all information that he could through observation, then the immediate job would be done. But greater tasks lay before them. Individual survival and eventual victory.

He would not let Karamatsov destroy the world again.

He would soon have a grandson, carried in Madison's womb. Sarah, he knew, was pregnant—the test she had planned to take was a formality. He knew it, she knew it. And the other woman he loved—Natalia. There had to be a life for her—his own making had destroyed her life in part. He would not let the rest of it be destroyed. Paul and Annie would have happiness. Madison and Michael. He and Sarah—and then he looked at Natalia and he realized how very little he did know, could do.

In some ways, the most important issue of his life and he was powerless to cause anything but sorrow.

Her incredibly blue eyes, the skin so white and soft and beautiful—and a heart that was given to him. And he could not take it, no matter how much he wanted to take it, to touch her.

John Thomas Rourke walked on, Natalia beside him, the young man Jea breaking the trail, their path keeping to the shelter of overhanging rocks as best as possible. But where it would lead after that, he didn't know . . .

Michael had pretended rudeness, indifference, exhaustion—the man had stopped talking to him, Michael nodding successfully and not speaking. It was possible, if the man beside him were clever, that the man had guessed something was amiss.

Shooting their way out once the plane was landed would be a futile gesture, but better than surrendering to inevitable death or worse.

And now the aircraft was landing, Michael—knowing Hammerschmidt beside him was doing the same—watching the other technicians from the truck to see what to do next.

The two who had been on the opposite side of the truck stood up wearily and stretched, then started slowly climbing aboard the vehicle's left side.

Michael stood, tapping Hammerschmidt on the shoulder as though awakening him, then started up to the catwalk.

The man who had been seated beside him spoke—he called out the name, "Yuri?"

Michael licked his lips—he turned.

Michael closed his eyes.

In the man's right hand was a wrench—from a tool belt that the man and some of the others like him wore.

The man started for him, up the catwalk, swinging the wrench. Michael twisted around, kicking the man in the chin, Hammerschmidt diving upward for the catwalk, the technicians around him swamping him down.

Men in silver colored decontamination suits swarmed everywhere—over Hammerschmidt and toward the ladder leading to the catwalk, the plane jostling them as it taxied along, Michael ripping open the front of his decontamination suit and ripping one of the Beretta military pistols out of the leather.

But he stabbed his right hand with the pistol in it not toward the men in the decontamination suits, but toward the massive cannister at the center of the truck.

The technicians dropped back, edged as far from Michael and as close to the bulkhead as they could.

Hammerschmidt was up, in English saying, "Good thinking Michael—now what?"

Hammerschmidt drew his German pistol.

"Get those guys forward as near to the cockpit as you can—anybody steps outa line, shoot the tank here—we've got nothin' to lose."

"Agreed."

Hammerschmidt gestured with his pistol toward the tank, then gestured the silver decontamination suited men toward the front of the truck, toward the front of the aircraft.

Michael drew his second pistol, aiming it at the men opposite him on the left side of the tank.

They climbed down, joined the others. Michael edged forward along the catwalk, anxious eyes behind the face masks of the driver and his helper. Michael let himself grin and gestured with one of his pistols toward the cannister.

With the other pistol he waved them out of the truck cab. They obeyed, Michael peering through the rear window. Soviet trucks still used key started ignitions—it was nice to know. And the keys were in the ignition.

He had been driving a truck since his pre-teens.

He thought of Madison—she had been getting pretty good at it. He closed his eyes tight against the tears, no time for them now.

He opened his eyes.

Hammerschmidt's voice. "I suppose we back the truck out of here as soon as they open the cargo doors and then, as you Americans say, play it by a nose, hmm?"

"It's by ear—but by a nose might turn out appropriate—we'll see." And Michael started climbing down from the catwalk, to board the truck cab. "You see, we try to save our asses while we play it by ear in the hope that we'll come in first at least by a nose—anatomically very complicated."

The German commando captain laughed. "I like you, Michael Rourke."

"You're not so bad yourself, Otto Hammerschmidt. I'll drive this sucker, you shoot people, okay?"

"Okay—yes."

"I'll shoot a few people too, though—taught myself how to drive and shoot when I was a kid. When we opened these suits—well, if this cannister is leaking at all after five centuries in the desert and the stuff inside is half as deadly as I think it is—"

"We have precipitated our own eventual deaths."

"Well put. So—no sense farting around with these damned decontamination suits. Right?"

"Agreed, Michael," and Hammerschmidt stripped away his head gear and laughed as he inhaled. "To death, hmm?"

"How about to beating it?" Michael opined, stripping away his own head gear—and suddenly laughing too. "Let's get the wheel chocks out of the way."

Chapter Seventeen

The aircraft was at full stop—Michael could feel it, his mind racing to familiarize himself with the truck's dashboard—oil pressure gauges, oil temperature gauges, monitors for the shock absorption systems. He could hear the cargo doors opening.

"They won't be too eager to shoot at us with this cannister—if we can keep it between us and them."

"Agreed," Hammerschmidt nodded, his pistol in both fists, his body crouched between the front seat and the firewall, the windows of the vehicle on both sides rolled down. "But I wish I had more than this to shoot at them with."

Michael only nodded, ripping one of the Berettas from the leather, sliding it under his right thigh, butt out, ready to his right hand.

The vehicle had a manual transmission—he gathered as a concession to the heavy nature of the load it had been designed for and the terrain it was intended to successfully navigate.

Michael found reverse.

In the rearview mirror he could see what Hammerschmidt's words confirmed. "The cargo doors are opening, Michael."

Michael began revving the engine, trying to get the feel of its pulse, his left hand poised on the emergency brake release, his eyes straining into the mirror for the moment the cargo doors would be fully opened and the ramp dropped.

Almost.

"Nearly open, Michael!"

"We're gone!" Michael popped the emergency brake release as he stomped the gas pedal and let up on the clutch, the truck lurching, starting rearward but painfully slow it seemed, shouts rising from the men in the forward position of the fuselage. Michael looked forward for an instant—one of the decontamination suited technicians was jumping for the driver's side door. Michael freed his left hand of the wheel and punched the man in the face through the open window. The technician fell back, the interior of the mask smudging with blood over the nose.

Michael put the pedal to the floorboard, the truck moving faster now, his left fist locked on the top of the wheel, his right fist on the gearshift, the light here gray, darkening, his face and hands already feeling the cold of the air temperature.

Men—armed, but wearing decontamination suits— were running up the ramp. The crack of Hammerschmidt's pistol, roughly like a 9mm Parabellum. A second shot—two of the decontamination suited armed men went down. More were running, clambering aboard the truck trailer.

"Shoot over the top of the cannister, then aim your pistol at the cannister—and keep as low as you can!"

"Right!"

Another pistol shot, but no answering fire from the guards swarming over the truck trailer now, the vehicle halfway down the ramp, a cold wind whipping a fine spray of snow across the air. In the rear window of the cab, Michael could see the armed guards falling back now, climbing down from the trailer and the cannister it carried—of what, he wondered—and running as though terrified.

The trailer was starting to jackknife. Michael cut in the brake, working the transmission into first, taking the cab forward, some of the silver suited technicians bunching back now. The rear end started straightening, and Michael hauled into reverse again, locking the wheel as he stomped the gas pedal. He shot a glance at Hammerschmidt—the German commando was still aiming his pistol at the massive cannister behind them.

The ramp leading into the rear of the cargo lifted. Michael could just barely see that the rear end of the massive vehicle was onto the ramp, feel the drag now as the weight of the machine started pulling back—but he kept his foot hard to the gas pedal, a bounce and a lurch now, cries of panic from around him, curses—no detailed knowledge of Russian would have been required. The truck was on the edge of being out of control, but he fought the wheel, keeping onto the ramp, the icy wind now penetrating the cab of the truck with the windows full open.

A man in full decontamination suit and battle gear cast his rifle aside and lurched toward the hood of the truck cab as Michael reversed past him, grabbing the Beretta under his right thigh, stabbing it through the window as his thumb worked off the safety. He fired, then again, both slugs impacting the man's center of mass, the body rocking back, slamming against the fuselage, then toppling over the side of the ramp.

He used the safety to drop the hammer, but still held the weapon in his right fist—his hand was large enough to work the knob on the floor mounted stick.

"Michael—they're forming up in a circle around us."

"Keep your pistol aimed at the cylinder—and hang

on!" Michael wrenched the wheel, but prematurely, the truck cab's front wheels still partially on the ramp. There was a sickening lurch, Michael fighting the wheel, still grasping his pistol, the truck cab nearly overturning and shouts and orders echoing from all around him. The cab seemed to rock on the left wheels, then righted itself, Michael stomping the gas pedal again, not caring now if the rear end jackknifed—the more unpredictable his driving, the more disorganized his Russian opposition would be. He raked the wheel hard right, then hard left, the rear end fishtailing side to side across the snow, the left side of the trailer nearly impacting the ramp leading back into the cargo lifter.

The Beretta held between his thumb and first finger, the last three fingers of his right hand found the shift knob, Michael hammered the brake with the heel of his right foot, his toe smashing down the accelerator as his left foot stomped the clutch. The cab seemed airborne for an instant, the trailer swaying side to side, rocking on its suspension. He slammed the transmission into first as his foot eased the gas pressure, then stomped the gas almost to the floor.

In the rearview, across the length of the cannister, he could see men running, rifles at high port, looking like moon men from a science fiction novel more than living Russian soldiers in silver decontamination suits. There were troops without decontamination gear, but they were hanging back.

Michael's left foot found the clutch and he depressed the gas full to the floor, double clutching as he upshifted, hammering the pedal to the floor now in second, the truck sluggish still, but moving faster at least. Behind it, visible in the rearview great breakers of snow plowing upward on either side and behind them, the decontamination suited men were still running after them.

Michael stabbed the Beretta out the window, careful to keep his line of fire at a tangent to the metal cylinder they hauled, firing randomly, hoping to hold them back. Some fell back—but most of the Soviet personnel kept running after the truck.

There was a shot from his right—his heart went to his mouth—but Hammerschmidt hadn't shot into the cylinder, but instead killed a man climbing up to the right side trailer catwalk.

Third gear—Michael hammered down the accelerator, the truck starting to gather momentum now.

A jeep-like vehicle dead in front of them skidded to a stop, the decontamination suited driver and a second man jumping from it, running for their lives.

No time to swerve away from the vehicle—Michael shouted, "Watch out!" and double clutched down into second, the transmission grinding, the engine sounding as if it would over-rev, the nose of the truck cab impacting the vehicle, bouncing it upward, the vehicle nearly crashing down along the hood, a scraping sound of metal against metal as Michael up-shifted, past it now, a fireball belching skyward, black and orange, the heat searing for an instant against the bare flesh of his left hand and the left side of his face—if it affected the cannister—

Fourth gear now, APCs starting to move, more of the jeep-like vehicles and two motorcycles starting in pursuit.

For the first time, Michael took an instant to assess their surroundings. Subarctic. Snowy. Mountainous. Trees in the distance—but nothing that looked like an entrance to an underground city of any sort, let alone the Underground City of the Soviet leadership.

The motorcycles were coming fast now as Michael cut the wheel left, aiming toward the mouth of a valley ahead of him. The motorcycles were nearly even with the trailer now—"Shit," Michael snarled. "Pray they were able to monitor that tracking signal on the radio set," and Michael looked again behind them.

The motorcycles—one man on each machine—had to be dead even with the trailer, hugging the sides. He could barely make out the man on the right, the one on the left reaching up for the catwalk—he would jump for the cannister.

"Otto!"

Hammerschmidt leaned out the cab window, then tucked back. "I cannot shoot—the one on my side is too close to the cannister—if I missed."

Michael reached to his left calf, grabbing the handle of the Life Support System II knife he hadn't yet transferred back to his belt. He drew the blade from the sheath. "Here—don't lose it. I couldn't replace it."

"I'll try not to."

Hammerschmidt took the knife and wrenched open the passenger side door, the cold wind now doubly strong, Michael's body trembling with the chill. And Hammerschmidt was gone, swinging out onto the running board. Michael glanced back, could see Hammerschmidt clambering along between the cab and the trailer, then leaping down to the level of the trailer and, catching hold of the cylinder, skidding against it. But he had the knife still, hacking with it at the fingers of the man trying to grab for the catwalk. Even over the roar of the slipstream, Michael could hear the scream as there was a sudden spray of blood and in the right sideview, the motorcycle seemed to disappear, the man with it, then the truck lurching slightly. It had crushed both man and machine.

The man on the left was onto the catwalk, the

motorcycle spinning out into the snow.

The man was edging forward. There was a blur in the rearview—Hammerschmidt. The German captain of commandoes had tackled the man across the cannister, driving the man down to the catwalk, the knife flashing in the dying sun for an instant, then driving downward.

It seemed like less than a second later and the body of the man in the decontamination suit was launched from the catwalk, into the air, then tumbled into the snow.

Hammerschmidt waved that he was all right, Michael finding fifth gear, on a comparative straightaway now, translating mentally kilometers into miles, realizing that the speedometer was telling him the truck was flat out on a level straightaway at a little less than sixty.

The APCs seemed to be matching his speed from a distance, but the jeep-like vehicles were closing.

He had no idea where they would go, how they would evade the Russians—if they could evade the Russians. Where did you hide a truck this size?

He was freezing cold, one level somewhere inside him afraid, but too preoccupied with staying alive to let the fear concern him.

Michael Rourke kept driving.

Chapter Eighteen

Jea pointed straight ahead beyond a natural wall of rock, and said something that although Rourke could not fathom the word, the meaning behind it seemed evident—"There it is."

"Tell Jea to keep down and keep him between us," John Rourke almost whispered, the SSG slung diagonally across his back, the one spent round replaced in the five-round rotary magazine, the scope and rifle checked for damage, neither having sustained any. His pistols long since reloaded and reholstered, in his gloved hands now was the M-16.

He moved ahead, hugging his back to the rocks as he crossed around the wall, not knowing at all what lay beyond.

He stopped as he came to the other side.

There was a tunnel extending for perhaps five hundred yards, like a chimney on its side, thrusting from the base of a huge mountain.

He let the rifle fall to his side on its sling, taking up the Bushnell armored 8x30s, taking them from the black zippered case, removing the lens caps, setting the subjective lenses before his eyes, working the center focus knob.

Greenhouses. No sign of electrical power terminals—likely underground. An airfield more expansive

140

than any he had ever seen. But he reminded himself this was an airfield to serve a nation. Hangars dotted the edges of the airfield and he was unable to tell what numbers of planes there might be—he saw a few helicopters, a few long range bomber-type aircraft, smaller fighter planes. Hardly the force of a nation.

His suspicions were confirmed.

Natalia, beside him now, echoed them. "Vladmir—he is staging troops—"

"For a coup."

He felt her body press close against him and he held her tightly . . .

They had worked their way down along the face of the wall of rock to find a better vantage point from which to observe the main and so far apparently solitary entrance to the Underground City. They lay on the rocks now, with the declining visibility almost too poor for accurate observation. But there was a need to know. By morning he would have to contact Captain Hartman, to alert the Germans to the situation and if he were to discover some means by which the situation could be capitalized upon, he had to know all he could learn.

There had been some comings and goings through the tunnel, Rourke still unable to see the actual entryway. Trucks, smaller vehicles reminiscent of jeeps, a vehicle that seemed to be some sort of snow cat. Rourke imagined a parking area for the larger vehicles, within the tunnel perhaps or just beyond. The tunnel's width was the width of an eight lane highway, its height the height of a four story building. It seemed constructed of concrete—perhaps something more modern. The mountain would be immune to weapons strikes except direct hit nuclear and the tunnel seemed nearly as invulnerable.

He began to strip out of his backpack as night

eventually fell, telling Natalia, "I have to go down there."

"I know that—I can go with you."

"No. You know as much as I do. If for some reason I don't come back, get on the radio to Hartman and give him all of it, work out a best guess scenario for him, give him something to act upon besides military infeasibility. And if I don't come back—well—see if you can get the Germans to do something to help Jea and his people. And—"

"Yes, John Rourke."

"I love you—I'm sorry it couldn't have been different for us."

"I know."

Rourke closed his eyes and drew her toward him, kneeling there with her, face to face, her head coming to rest against his chest. Natalia, her voice sounding muffled with the scarf worn over her mouth and nose against the cold, because of her head being so close to him, spoke. "I was on an assignment once in India. I brought back a beautiful sari for myself and a smattering of the philosophy of transmigration of souls. When we do die, if they were right at all, maybe sometime we can be together again after death, in a new life."

"Shh," Rourke murmured, just holding her . . .

He had taken to the air over the fleeing truck and could follow it easily now despite the darkness which had swept over the ground below him—the headlights, bouncing and weaving across the rugged terrain, the headlights of the stolen truck and the pursuit vehicles which chased it.

He had seen the face of the man behind the wheel—it was Michael Rourke. The eyes, the profile, the hairline, the thrust of the jaw.

The other man with Michael Rourke was unrecognizable to him—he imagined one of the Germans with whom the Rourkes had allied.

Several things worried him and he spoke aloud of them to Krakovski who shared the helicopter with him, piloted it. Into the teardrop microphone before his lips, he said, "If Michael Rourke is here—and that was Michael Rourke unless John Rourke has lost the touch of gray in his hair, has abandoned his sunglasses, those cigars of his—but if Michael Rourke is here, then his father cannot be far away. I know John Rourke—he would not insert his son into a dangerous situation without great cause without being nearby to assist him."

"But Comrade Marshal," Ivan Krakovski began, the voice soft in Karamatsov's ear, despite the rush of the air around them, the muted whirring of the rotor blades. "He is driving toward the Underground City."

"Yes—he transports the cylinder there for us."

"But Comrade Marshal—what is in the cylinder?"

Vladmir Karamatsov looked at Krakovski. "Picture the Underground City with more than half its complement of defensive personnel driven mad, Ivan, and likely slaughtering the other half for us. That is what is contained in the cylinder. Order that the great tires of the truck be shot out—we must risk it because Michael Rourke drives the truck there too soon for us and he must be stopped. I wish him taken alive—the other, the German, can be killed or not. It does not matter. And stay well away from the vehicle in the event that the cannister is struck."

"Yes, Comrade Marshal," and Karamatsov listened as Krakovski switched frequencies and gave the order. It would be very interesting to possess Michael Rourke as a prisoner . . .

* * *

Bjorn Rolvaag's dog lay asleep. Bjorn Rolvaag did not.

Captain Hartman had returned less than two hours ago and seemed exhausted, as though he should have fallen into a deep sleep, slept and slept away the night. But instead he had ordered that they move out and they had, moving by the strange vehicles John Rourke had called snow cats.

It was a lonely time for Rolvaag—he spoke no English, no German. And after the forced march into the rocky, mountainous area Hartman had chosen for their encampment, even his dog was too tired to listen to him.

So Rolvaag sat quietly, holding his great staff, contemplating this turn in his life.

He trusted the German named Hartman and assumed they had moved for a valid reason, and that John Rourke and Natalia Tiemerovna would return eventually he trusted as well—or nearly so.

But this was what he had become embroiled in—it was a strange war.

His nation of Iceland had known nearly five centuries of peace. He did not blame the Rourkes for bringing the war to Iceland—it would have come whether they had come or not. It was not a war of Iceland, but a war of the entire world, a war that was older than the five centuries of peace his people had enjoyed.

He had always considered himself a guardian of what was correct—not so much a guardian of the law. So it was not strange being here, defending what was correct against what was vile.

He had struck up friendships with some of the Germans, even though no common tongue was shared among them. A smile, a handclasp—it was all that it took, and then the will to back up the smile and the handclasp with kindness and respect. When the time came to meet the Russians in battle, he would utilize his staff, his sword and his hands. Other weapons were alien to him and he left these other weapons to those to whom such things were not alien. He would fight as he had always learned to fight.

But he had never had to fight in all his life until the Russians had invaded his home.

Some day, when the Russians were defeated, there would again be a dearth of need to fight and he could return to roaming the snows beyond Hekla, to the warmth of a campfire with the dog that slept beside him.

He folded himself and his staff into the blankets and rolled onto his side beside the sleeping animal and his right hand touched the animal's neck and only barely consciously began to stroke the fur there.

Rolvaag closed his eyes, inviting sleep to come . . .

John Rourke ran hard, stripped of his excess gear, wearing the night black smock over his parka rather than the snow smock he had worn earlier—but the garment was one and the same, reversible—he mentally saluted German ingenuity as he dropped to a shadowy depression some hundred yards from the nearest edge of the Soviet airfield.

He had encountered electronic countermeasures, but easily defeated them. Neither the Underground City, it appeared, nor the airfield complex, had been constructed with security in mind. Security from what? would have been the operative philosophy.

It paid to plan ahead. Anticipation was a pl phy Vladmir Karamatsov pursued but did no that well, Rourke had realized early in his encounters with the man.

That he had failed to verify his own work, to give Karamatsov the head shot which would have finished him, was something John Rourke constantly considered—he, John Rourke, had failed to plan ahead and the results had been disastrous, cost lives, nearly the life of his son, his daughter, his wife, Natalia, whom he loved as deeply as any of them, of Paul, of himself.

To his feet, running again, brushing the white snow from the shadow colored black of his clothing, the assault rifle in both fists at high port, the yawning cavity of the entrance tunnel still hundreds of yards off. He dropped behind one of the snow cats that had been left out, if not for the night, conveniently long enough that he could use it.

His eyes scanned to right and left in the night. There was little moon, the sky heavy with clouds. The effect of prolonged sleeplessness was telling on him, but only a bit.

He started to his feet, out of the crouch, but froze— there were lights in the distance, specks only of light— but they were coming toward him.

Rourke threw himself to the ground, working the M-16's safety tumbler to auto.

Chapter Nineteen

They were coming with motorcycles again, getting perilously close and Michael cranked down the window. "Shoot 'em, Otto!"

Hammerschmidt fired, but the motorcycles in the right side mirror—they had been called West Coast mirrors sometimes, he remembered absently from his readings—simply dropped back, a momentary flash of sparks as Hammerschmidt's bullet apparently harmlessly contacted metal and richocheted.

In the left side mirror, he could see a second rider, in the man's hand a pistol perhaps—in the darkness and the intermittent flashing of headlights from the pursuit vehicles, it was hard to tell.

Michael Rourke's mind raced—the tires. "They're trying for the tires. Probably have armor piercing loads in their pistols. Watch out!"

"There's something up ahead—Michael, it looks like an airfield, I think."

Michael had seen it a moment earlier. But there was no time to worry over it. The Beretta was in his right fist tight, the transmission in fifth, the highest gear, the gasoline pedal to the floor, the gasoline tank nearly drained, helicopter gunships overhead in pursuit. "Shit," he hissed.

The motorcycle on his side was coming again. He

twisted a little behind the wheel, stabbing the Beretta out the window, firing once, then again, then again and again. The motorcyclist hugged to his machine.

A pistol—Michael could see it, twisting closer to the window, firing a double tap from the Beretta—at least one of the shots was a hit, the cyclist twisting in his saddle, the bike impacting one of the trailer's massive wheels, then bouncing, airborne, a scream in the air behind him.

To his right, Otto Hammerschmidt was firing again, "Damn—I missed him." Another shot, louder than a 9mm or the German equivalent. The truck cab lurched. "Hit a tire—" Another shot from Hammerschmidt, then another of the louder shots and Michael's steering started to go, the truck cab swerving wildly, Hammerschmidt firing again. "Got him—but too late!"

"Got him or the bike?"

"The man."

"The motorcycle survive?"

"I think so—what?"

"When I say, jump for it, get the machine—I'll cover you." Michael's right foot pumped the brake, the heel only, his toe working the gas pedal as he double-clutched, downshifting, his fists locked tight on the steering wheel, the Beretta nearly empty back under his thigh.

Speed was dropping—maybe too fast he thought, the trailer started to jacknife on him. Michael did the only thing he could, cutting the wheel hard right, then snapping it left all the way; the cab started to spin, the trailer fishtailing behind them, starting to go over. "Jump, Otto! I'm right behind ya!"

Hammerschmidt's door flew open, Hammerschmidt looking back once as Michael glanced toward him, then jumping into the night. The trailer was starting to go over, the cab starting to rock left. Michael grabbed his pistol, held the wheel as long as he could, edging right, then loosed the wheel as the cab started to roll now as Michael threw himself from it, impacting the snow hard, rolling out of it, his right shoulder aching, the Beretta still in his right fist. His left hand found the second pistol as he came out of the roll, to his knees, ripping the second Beretta from the leather, working the safety off, firing both pistols toward the nearest of the Soviet vehicles, one of the jeep-like pursuit cars. He heard the shattering of glass—but then he heard nothing else from it, a screeching of metal, tearing, twisting, rending sounds filling the night as he looked behind him. The massive trailer was flipping over, the cab breaking away from it, launched skyward, the cab's gas tanks suddenly exploding as Michael threw himself face down into the snow, his hands, still clutching his pistols, shielding his head and neck.

As he looked up, above the crackle of flames, he heard the pulse of a motor, and Hammerschmidt's voice, "Michael!"

To his feet, running, the pistol in his right fist empty, the one in his left fist spitting toward the fleeing Soviet vehicles.

He jumped into the long saddle behind Hammerschmidt, "Roll it!"

The bike lurched ahead—in the distance, Michael could see some sort of impossibly long, impossibly large tunnel—and there was gunfire coming from it, toward them. Michael looked back—the driver of one of the jeep-like vehicles vaulted from his seat, his machine spinning out, crashing into a chunk of burning debris from the cab, rolling over, itself on fire now.

Hammerschmidt aimed the motorcycle toward a rock wall that formed the base of a mountain perhaps a half mile distant.

It had been bravado before, removing the decontamination suits—once the integrity of the suits had been broken, the suits were useless anyway. But now—if the cannister had leaked or cracked. He wondered what possible death awaited them.

Chapter Twenty

John Rourke ran—in the momentary glow of flames when the cab of the enormous truck had exploded, there had been light—and the face he had seen of the man jumping aboard a motorcycle behind another man, a man with pistols blazing from each hand, had been identical to his own face. It was his son's face.

John Rourke had run into the open to make the shots that had taken out the driver of the jeep-like vehicle which had been about to close with Michael and the other man with him, and now suddenly he was in the middle of a small war. Vehicles streamed from the entrance to the Underground City, helicopters airborne in the night sky, firing toward the vehicles, other vehicles approaching the trailer of the huge vehicle, the trailer overturned, a cylinder larger than the kind used for underground storage of gasoline before the Night of The War half in, half out of the trailer, men in gleaming silver decontamination suits milling around it.

Rourke dodged a vehicle coming from the Underground City, a man beside the driver firing an errant shot toward him. Rourke, instead of returning fire, took a running leap, crashing down into the rear of the vehicle. The man with the pistol opened fire.

Rourke swatted the pistol away as it discharged, the top of the head of the man behind the wheel exploding away from them, the vehicle careening crazily now. Rourke's left fist closed over the Soviet pistol, his right fist crossing his opponent's jawline, snapping the head back hard, Rourke losing the pistol now, his left fist catching the tip of the jaw and rocking it left and back. There was an audible crack as the neck broke. Rourke lunged for the wheel, his left fist closing over it.

He started to push the headshot man from the driver's seat and to the ground—but he didn't. There was a flash of memory now—Michael had been coatless and so had the other man with Michael aboard the motorcycle.

Instead, Rourke shoved the body right, the jeep-like vehicle under control now, Rourke sliding over the back of the seat, into position behind the wheel, his feet finding the pedals, his right foot hammering down the accelerator. The vehicle had veered away from the gradually escalating war there before the tunnel mouth of the Underground City, Russians fighting Russians, Rourke realized. And whatever was in the cannister was valuable enough that Karamatsov was holding to the battle. In the distance now, illuminated for an instant by the light of a flare, he could see the outline of a workhorse helicopter, a crane dangling down from beneath it.

It had to be Karamatsov—and some ultimate bid for ultimate power.

John Rourke started toward the wall of rock—he had seen Michael and the other man aboard the motorcycle going that way, and Natalia and the young primitive named Jea would likely still be there as well.

His prospects had increased really—it was sometimes good to look on the bright side. With Russians

152

fighting Russians, security would be heightened at the Underground City, but at least they would be too busy to bother looking for him and for the others. Michael was a good fighter. The man with Michael was likely a German commando of some type. Perhaps there were more of the Germans, all the more to supplement Hartman's force. And there were two vehicles now—gasoline could be stolen if necessary. He reminded himself—gasoline was an anachronism. Synth-fuel.

The mountain wall was getting nearer and he cut the headlights on the vehicle he drove—he could see well enough, the inverse of his light sensitivity, in cases like this a blessing.

On a realistic note, he thought, perhaps things weren't looking up that dramatically, but it would be good to see his son Michael again, very soon . . .

Natalia Anastasia Tiemerovna raised her hands to her mouth as though to stifle a cry—but she made no cry. John Rourke had begun to weep, and then Michael started to cry, and father and son embraced each other and she loved them both and she closed her eyes, visions of Madison, pretty Madison—dead now and gone. And the baby. Tears flooded her eyes and through the blur of her own vision, she could see Jea, staring oddly at all of them, and the German commando Captain—Hammerschmidt?—with his back slowly turning to them, his hands going up to cover his face.

She could no longer help herself—she ran to both men—John and Michael—and put her arms up, her hands touching at their heads, her head leaning against their bodies, against their interwoven arms.

Chapter Twenty-one

Otto Hammerschmidt had watched the Russian woman—he had heard of her, heard of her a great deal. She was as beautiful as he had been told—even more so. After withdrawing higher into the rocks when she had called out to them, following her and the strange looking young wildman, then the famous John Rourke had arrived, the Herr Doctor in a stolen Russian vehicle, his spirits seeming high. And Michael had said simply, "A Soviet suicide patrol attacked Hekla—I tried to stop them. Madison shielded me with her body and she died, Dad—Madison and the baby—they're gone," and Hammerschmidt had watched an outpouring of affection and love like none he had ever seen before.

He drove the motorcycle now, wearing his stolen Soviet arctic gear with the bloodstains the Herr Doctor had apologized for, the Herr Doctor's voice tight with grief, strange sounding.

John Rourke and Michael Rourke sat in the back of the Soviet vehicle, the Russian woman and the wildboy in the front seat. The Russian woman never looked from her driving. Both Rourke men looked straight ahead.

What could anyone say, Hammerschmidt thought. He remembered the death of his father when he had been but a young man. He could think of it now and without knowing it begin to cry . . .

John Rourke spoke. "Whatever the Russians have in that cannister is evidently a weapon that is either chemical or biological. Michael—you and Captain Hammerschmidt appear healthy except for being a little tired. But it could be some biological weapon the effects of which might not appear for some time. It could be so contagious all of us have it. But I doubt that. I think, from the way the two of you described it, that Karamatsov was just being cautious, and the suits would only have been necessary were the tank to have sprung a leak. We have no reason to suppose it didn't, but there's no reason to suppose it did either." Rourke looked at his watch. "In a very little while, Captain Hartman will be listening for our radio transmission. He was originally supposed to add fourteen to whatever number I gave him and use that system to determine our next time of broadcast. But that was based on our having monitored Soviet communications and determined the best time for broadcast. We haven't done that yet—and there's no time now. We have a code—your Westphalia Two, Captain," and Rourke looked at Hammerschmidt. "But the Soviets will be able to break that given enough time. So—we'll arrange a meeting point, as fast as possible, and conduct the rest of our planning in person. If the Russians are battling among themselves, we can use that to our advantage. Put together whatever force we can and attack Karamatsov while he's fighting the forces of the Underground City. I'd venture to say whatever sort of weapon that tank contains is for use against the Underground City, not against us. We're going to have to wait until he uses it in order to determine its nature and how to prevent his using it on us. I haven't figured that out yet.

"The important thing," Rourke said slowly, his voice almost a whisper, the glow of the lamp around which they all sat illuminating the rock overhang beneath which they had taken shelter, the faces of all to whom he spoke, except Natalia, in shadow, "is that we get together whatever response team we can and do something while Karamatsov will be at his weakest. Karamatsov has to be destroyed."

Michael's voice came from the darkness. "I'm doing it."

Natalia whispered, "It should be me."

"I should have made sure that first time—Madison—" and he felt his throat tighten as he looked toward the shadow of his son.

"It's not your fault, Dad."

"The important thing," Rourke whispered, "is that Karamatsov dies. If there's already dissension among the Russian leadership and Karamatsov is out of the picture, the disorganization should be greater. And that'll work to our advantage. If you want him that badly, then I hope you get him, Michael."

"But the neutralization of Karamatsov takes precedence over which of us accomplishes it," Michael's voice came back from the darkness. "That's what you're saying—right?"

"That's what I'm saying. Whoever can kill him must kill him."

"What is your intent, Herr Doctor."

Rourke looked toward Hammerschmidt. "In our time, Captain, when films were a popular medium of

156

entertainment, at some crucial moment someone or another would always say, 'I have a plan'. Well—I have a plan. Our two best candidates for observing what goes on out there are you, Captain, and Natalia. Natalia knows the Russian way of thinking, way of planning, better than any of us. And Vladmir Karamatsov was her husband—"

"Is, John."

"No—he stepped out of the human community a long time ago. No—but with the two of you, we have the best advantage. I was never a military man—"

"You are too modest, Herr Doctor."

"Not modest—practical. Between the two of you, we have the best chance of finding out what they're doing. Michael and I will arrange to meet with Captain Hartman and then contact your unit, Captain Hammerschmidt. We'll attempt to get whatever personnel we can in here quick. We can utilize Jea's people as scouts for us—they know this terrain better than anyone including the Russians and should have a vested interest in helping if it can be developed. Their people have been taken prisoner for experimentation or just slaughtered, it seems from what he tells us. We'll all rendezvous at a preselected site and time, take what intelligence data we have and formulate an attack plan."

"I could get inside, John—perhaps—"

"No," Rourke told her. "No one goes inside until we better understand the nature of Karamatsov's new weapon." And Rourke shot his cuff again, turned the upper portion of his wrist toward the lantern and read the time. The horizon beyond the rock overhang was gray already. It would be a stormy day, but what light there would be seemed almost intent upon coming quickly, infiltrating beneath the layers of cloud. "Natalia and Hammerschmidt, put your heads together on the Westphalia Two code—he knows it better than either of us. Work a rendezvous site and time with Hartman as soon as terrain and situation will allow. Give him very few details—less for the Russians to intercept and decode eventually. Michael and I can refuel the four-wheel-drive vehicle with the cans it was carrying and throw another gallon or so of fuel into the motorcycle. Whatever it'll take."

"Yes, John."

Rourke stood up—somewhere along the line, he would have to schedule some sleep.

He started off into the shadows . . .

Annie Rourke opened her eyes—Paul sat staring almost blankly. She looked up at him, her head on his lap. "How long did I sleep?"

"About nine hours. I just woke up a few minutes ago," and she felt his legs shift beneath her head. She started to rise, but he touched his hand to her face and whispered to her, "Just a little stiff—I'm fine. You didn't look restless the few times I woke up."

"I slept fine—whatever danger—I didn't see any more."

"That's good, Annie—that's very good."

"You need a shave."

"You're probably right," he smiled, bending over her, Annie raising her face, Paul touching his lips to her forehead. She hugged the blanket more tightly about her. Despite the climate control, she felt cold somehow in the tent.

They were alone in the tent that was headquarters "building" for the small German outpost here. She wondered what time it was. "What time is it?"

"A little after six common time—which is just about right for here according to the sun as best I can figure."

"Thank you for putting up with me—dragging you out here, I mean."

"I love you—now, young woman—sit up—because if you don't, I might not make it to the bathroom on time—gotta go—"

Annie didn't budge an inch. "How badly do you have to go?"

Paul, with faked roughness, shoved her head up and stood, "Badly!"

Annie sat up, watching him as he started toward their small quarters at the far side of the tent. There was a perfectly serviceable, even comfortable looking air lofted mattress in there. But she had wanted to be awake lest there would be word from her father and Natalia and then she had consented to putting her head on Paul's lap and closing her eyes and the next thing she had known it had been morning.

She realized she was smiling—thinking about Paul. She rolled the words on her tongue. "Husband. Wife." She liked both sounds . . .

It was not the way he had planned it—thanks once again to someone named Rourke.

The bulk of his force fought a holding action, containing the occupants of the Underground City and sealing off the airfield from their use. This was bad, because many of his soldiers had wives and families inside the Underground City and the longer the battle protracted, the more their fears for loved ones would grow and the less reliable they would become.

It was anticipating such as this—but for different reasons—which had prompted him to call in Krakovski originally from the field to assist in the Egyptian operation.

With Krakovski's arrival, there had been the perfect excuse to form around Krakovski an elite corps of men and some women whom he could trust to remain loyal regardless of what should occur.

And this elite corps—not his old KGB Elite Corps, but similar in composition—was not at the front lines, but he had kept it with him instead.

Once the helicopter crane had removed the cannister from the entrance to the Underground City, Karamatsov had personally supervised its inspection. In full decontamination gear he had checked each seam, the locking cap over the main valve. There had been no damage. It was the sort of situation that persons who believed in that sort of thing would call miraculous. Vladmir Karamatsov doubted that God would aid his endeavor, however.

He stood, watching the yellow gray line of horizon, the deeper gray of clouds. It would snow today—heavily.

He looked away from the horizon, to Krakovski and the hundred members of his new elite corps. He began to speak. "Today, you shall participate in the grand design of the future, Comrades." It was cold, the wind stiff, but he was sure they could hear him. From the small table that had been set outside his tent by his aide, he raised a small gleaming metallic cylinder, a perfect miniature of the huge cylinder.

"This tiny cylinder, Comrades, is our key to this glorious future. It, and others like it, will be filled from the tank we extricated from the sands of Egypt, the tank which we fought so successfully to save last night. A gas, Comrades—colorless, odorless, and tasteless, a gas which shall be introduced to the ventilation system of the Underground City, a gas unlike any ever used before in warfare. Had it not been for our enemies alerting the Underground City, the task which awaits you would have been easier. The gas cannisters could easily have been smuggled into the Underground City and radio activated as was my original plan. But that cannot be, now, Comrades. Some of you may remember that prior to our taking to the field to intercept the Eden Project upon its return, the last of the greenhouses was completed. Besides the water pipes and the electrical conduit running from inside the Underground City to each greenhouse, there is a third pipe, my comrades. This pipe feeds directly into the ventilation system of the Underground City. In teams of fire and maneuver, you will penetrate to the greenhouse sites with the appropriate number of cannisters. Even now as I speak the cannisters are being filled for you. You will mate the cannister intake valve to the terminus of the third pipe. You will be shown plans of the greenhouses to know how to find the proper terminus. You will not yet open the valves of the cannisters to release the gas into the pipes. At the base of each cannister," and he tapped the base, "you will see a second valve. To this valve you will attach a small length of hose which will be provided you. The other end will be attached to the blower units inside the greenhouses and the blower units will then be reversed. The blower will begin pumping air through the cannister into the pipeline. At this time, Comrades, you will open the cannister valves and the Underground City will be flooded with gas, the defenders rendered not only useless, but allies to our task of conquest."

Krakovski stepped forward from his position at the head of the hundred, shouting, "Three cheers for the Comrade Marshal—Hip—Hip!"

And as the cheers rang, Vladmir Karamatsov turned to stare at the horizon—the symbolism of the dawn of a new day. It would doubtless be included in young Krakovski's writings of this new beginning for the planet. But Krakovski was not the only one among them who could write. Vladmir Karamatsov promised himself that some day, he too would write—Krakovski's epitaph. No man—or woman—could be trusted with power.

Chapter Twenty-two

Natalia Anastasia Tiemerovna had elected to ride behind Captain Otto Hammerschmidt, her arms loosely about his waist as he took the motorcycle to the far side of the entrance into the Underground City, the side most directly opposite the airfield.

They had dismounted and camouflaged the motorcycle, then cautiously advanced to the farthest edge of the rocks, before and beneath them a battlefield.

Defensive shields of what appeared to be some lightweight but dense metal armor had been erected on both sides of the entrance tunnels, spreading backward in arcs, forming a horn linking into the sides of the mountain itself. Artillery of the conventional kind and also of some type with which she was not at all familiar but Hammerschmidt guessed could perhaps be energy weapons were emplaced behind the barricades, men and (she supposed) women at the barricades, machinegun and motor emplacements at strategic locations there as well.

Blocking the tunnel entrance were three of the most massive tanks she had ever seen, larger by far than the United States or Soviet tanks of the era immediately precursing the Night of The War.

But bigger did not always mean better, she told herself.

Periodically, the tanks would fire—conventional shells it seemed, utilizing high explosives, but the artillery did not fire. A reserve, she thought, or perhaps limited duration capabilities.

The greenhouses John had first noted, some of them partially demolished, lay at a tangent to the entrance to the city and the new fortifications. On the opposite tangent was the airfield. Two of the hangar buildings smoldered, apparently burned to the ground. Either there was not the time or the will to extinguish the fires during the night or early morning.

At the far side of the airfield were some three dozen helicopter gunships and behind these, fighter aircraft, but fewer than a dozen as best she could count. Shields similar to those utilized at the tunnel entrance to the Underground City were erected as a barrier bisecting the field at almost the exact center of its length, behind these shields artillery identical to that she had already noted used by the defenders of the Underground City, but the pieces fewer in number.

Men, however, were in greater abundance here, and machinegun emplacements were less spread and the result seemed an impenetrable killing zone against any kind of assault on foot.

Tanks—some few massive like those at the main entrance, but the bulk of more conventional size—were set facing the main entrance and main defenses, but some two thousand yards back along the length of the valley floor.

A third attack line was angled upward with its extremity less than a thousand yards from the entrance to the Underground City, the greenhouses approximately equidistant between attackers and defenders.

With binoculars, she abandoned the valley and began exploring the mountain itself. Gun emplacements atop the mountain in irregular arcs of a circle, but anti-aircraft defense it seemed quite plain, the mounts apparently not designed to allow even those guns which were on the valley side to be fired into the valley. Radar systems dotted the mountain top.

They had seen in the distance, that morning after broadcasting the message to Captain Hartman and separating from John, Michael and Jea, what could have been a communications tower. If it were, she had no doubt it and any others like it would be in the hands of her husband by now.

"Fraulein Major?"

"Yes?"

"I could not help but notice, Fraulein Major—you—you and the Herr Doctor Rourke. There is ahh—"

"No—there can't be." She turned her binoculars back to the valley floor, trying to catalogue numbers of troops and equipment in her mind.

"Forgive me, Fraulein Major—it was none of my affair."

Natalia didn't answer him.

Chapter Twenty-three

Rourke cut the engine as the jeep-like Soviet machine rolled down the incline into a smallish depression, not really large enough to be a valley. The coordinates were right for the meeting with Hartman.

Rourke locked the emergency brake and jumped to the ground, grabbing up his assault rifle, Michael going out the other side with the SSG in his fists, Jea still aboard the vehicle.

John Rourke gestured to Jea to accompany them, saying to Michael, "If the Russians did monitor our transmission, we're more mobile on foot considering the terrain. Let's get up into those rocks."

There was a nervous look to Jea's peculiar eyes and Rourke charged it off to bewilderment and lack of information, though Rourke had gotten Natalia to brief Jea before they had separated.

The young man climbed down awkwardly from the Soviet vehicle and fell in with them as Rourke and his son started upward. "I'm sorry," Rourke began.

"I know that."

"What are you going to do now—after this is all over?"

"I—ahh—there's a whole world out there, Dad—I don't know. I mean if I've got the patience for medical school—any of that. Maybe—ahh—just strike out on my own, see what there is to find."

"Better off on horseback than with a vehicle—

couldn't carry enough synth-fuel with you."

"I was thinking that. The Germans offered you some horses, right?"

"Yeah—Colonel Mann did. Good animals. Ahh—your mother—ahh—"

"She'll have the new baby—I didn't tell ya—but ahh—you and Mom were right. She had the test and she's pregnant. Should be sometime around the end of August. Anyway—I won't be gone forever, ya know?"

"Yeah—I know," John Rourke almost whispered. He stopped climbing into the rocks, stopped to look at Michael. "Ahh—I don't think any man could have a better son. I just wanted you to know that. I'm sorry for the world you inherited, Michael. I don't think anybody in our time really wanted it to come out like this."

"There's probably more life than we've found already—maybe I'll find some of it."

"Paul and I talked about that a little—going over the next mountain. But I don't suppose either of us can now. I don't envy how it came to this for you—but I kind of envy what you'll see. Once the baby's old enough to travel, well—"

"You mean the ages Annie and I were after the Night of The War?" And Michael smiled.

"Something like that," Rourke laughed a little. "Well—Sarah and I—your Mom and I—we might ahh—"

"And Paul and Annie too?"

"Sure—that'd be good."

Snow capped the mountains which ringed them, snow cascading in long rivers of white, cascading downward through the forests of pine and the sparser but significant numbers of hardwoods, frozen rivers waiting to go somewhere.

"What about Natalia?"

167

"I don't know—some things never change, do they."

"She's a good woman—I don't envy you—or her."

John Rourke closed his eyes, then opened them again, settling on a rock that was protected on three sides from sight by other rocks surrounding it, his vantage point affording him a view of the depression in the direction from which Hartman and his people should be coming.

"I never meant to be—"

"Unfaithful to Mom? You weren't."

"You love another woman as much as you love your wife—well—even if you don't touch her, there's a—"

"What?"

"I don't know. All I succeeded in doing was fucking up her life."

"Natalia'd never say that," Michael said quietly. "You gave her a new life. Maybe she's like me that way. You've got one major character failing, Dad—I can say it because I've got the same failing. You expect yourself to be perfect. We've got big egos."

John Rourke laughed. "We do, huh?"

"Yeah—we do," Michael grinned. Michael shifted the SSG to rest across his thighs. "Got a nice feel to it."

"There's another one back at the Retreat," and Rourke nodded toward the rifle.

"I'll take you up on it. But you can't blame yourself for being a human being. When you met Natalia, any rational man would have assumed Mom and Annie and I were dead. But you never did. You came after us, saved our lives—at a lot of personal expense. You know what I mean."

Rourke started to try to answer but he didn't have an answer. Michael kept talking instead. "I mean, what you did in finding us was at once self-sacrifice and selfishness. You searched for us because you wanted to find us—just like we searched for you. But at the same time you gave up Natalia. Is that why you got Mom pregnant? Honestly?"

"What? To keep myself from having to make a choice?"

"Maybe—something like that."

"Is that what you think?" John Rourke asked his son.

"No—I don't think that."

"Good—because it isn't why. At least I don't think it is. I didn't have any choice to make. Your mother is my wife. I can't put it into words. But I love your mother. I love Natalia. But the two loves are different. Four finest women I've ever known—your mother, Natalia, Annie, and your wife, Madison. I'll mourn Madison. Annie will grow away from me. Just as she should with Paul. Natalia's just like me. A survivor. She'll make a life for herself because that's the way to survive. Your mother and I'll be together as long as both of us live. We'll probably argue as long as we live, too. Never see eye-to-eye. I ahh—hell," and Rourke found one of his thin, dark tobacco cigars and bit down hard on it.

"I hope I never have to try and think like God," and Michael Rourke placed his arm across his father's shoulders.

John Rourke looked at his son. "I love you—very much."

"The three of us—all that time—I don't think we ever doubted that," Michael said softly.

John Rourke closed his eyes. "Thank you."

He opened his eyes—the rattle of equipment. It was either Hartman or a Soviet ambush.

169

Chapter Twenty-four

It was not the Russians.

They abandoned the Soviet vehicle after Hartman and his personnel thoroughly and quickly searched it. There had seemed to be an instant camaraderie struck up between Bjorn Rolvaag and Jea, Jea initially terrified by Rolvaag's dog, but warming to the animal so quickly it had almost seemed Jea and the dog had known each other throughout their lives.

Michael sat beside the driver of the snow cat, Rourke seated in the rear seat with Hartman, the snow cats taking them by a series of right angle jogs to the coordinates set for the predetermined rendezvous with Natalia and Captain Hammerschmidt.

While the Soviet vehicle had been searched, Hartman had broken radio silence to contact the base in Norway—Rourke had learned that his daughter and her husband, Paul Rubenstein, were waiting at the base. Hammerschmidt's men, led now by a Sergeant Dekker and in the company of a small force under Lieutenant Milton Schmidt were already enroute to the Urals, having monitored Hammerschmidt's tracking device sufficiently well to place the general geographic area.

The small force in Norway and Hammerschmidt's unit would consolidate with Hartman's small force of men—but the combined unit strength would be a token force at best against the Soviet numbers.

The commander of the Norway outpost was to contact Major Volkmer, commander of the Iceland base being erected outside Mt. Hekla, and Colonel Mann in Argentina. Rourke doubted any substantial force could be gotten into the Urals in time to do any good.

As they drove, Rourke recounted what he had seen and Michael conjectured on the nature of the substance contained in the cannister. "A bacteria wouldn't have survived five centuries in the desert—at least I don't think so."

"The nature of the bacteria, its reproductive rate, the amount of nutrient it might need—a considerable number of variables could come into play. Some mutant strain of bacteria might have properties that otherwise might be considered bizarre. But I agree—probably a gas."

The windows of the snow cat were steaming over, Hartman wiping one clear with the palm of his glove. "But what sort of gas—Herr Doctor—"

"During World War II, the German government had poison gas as did the allies—it was never used because each power felt that whoever utilized it first could expect retaliation in kind. That same philosophy, of course, carried over into post-war nuclear arsenal building. But germ warfare and gas warfare weren't abandoned. The Russians, we knew, were working on a wide range of chemical and biological agents. And so of course we were. Evidently, the cannister Karamatsov has unearthed in the desert was placed there some time after the Night of The War by some of his agents. Considering the size, I'd venture to say this isn't something Karamatsov had created for his own personal use, but rather something which had

171

been in readiness for another use which Karamatsov then expropriated. The Egyptian government would never have allowed the cannister to be buried in the first place if there had been a viable Egyptian government at the time—so it had to be after the Night of The War."

"Karamatsov was in charge of the KGB in the United States, though—"

"But before the Night of The War, Michael," Rourke continued, lighting the cigar he had been chewing on since a few moments before Hartman's arrival, "as Natalia could attest, Karamatsov had his hands everywhere. I bumped into him in South America. But he was a well-known Soviet agent at that time, having worked all over the world, and considerably with terrorists. He would have had the knowledge and contacts to get his hands on the cannister. Just as a scenario, and there's no reason to suppose it's correct, but it could have been a gas so terribly dangerous that the Soviets were planning to discard it, hence the durability of the cannister. Likely, it was already aboard a ship somewhere if that were the case, and ready to be dumped at sea. Karamatsov probably knew about it and when the Night of The War came and he suddenly had his wish—power—he took the cannister to use as a sort of ace-in-the-hole. But he couldn't have gotten something that size into North America without the Soviet Army learning about it and Natalia's uncle, General Varakov, learning of it through channels. Varakov wouldn't have stood for a poison gas stolen from his own government being the private ultimate weapon for Karamatsov. And Karamatsov was well aware of the theories regarding a conflagration of the atmosphere—which eventually came to pass—or some other disaster scenario. Which sparked his initial interest in the Womb, the cryogenic

172

chambers and the serum, which is what saved our lives.

"If it is a gas, and something extraordinarily deadly," Rourke said, looking at Michael, then at Hartman, "he put it away for a rainy day. And he put it away in Egypt because he didn't want it anywhere near him but he wanted it someplace easily located. Consider the possibilities. If a full blown nuclear winter had come about, it could have precipitated an ice age prematurely. As glaciers advance, as the icecaps increase in size, terrain features are altered. He wouldn't have wanted his cannister buried under tons of granite somewhere and to complicate that, polar shifts might have made terrestrial orienting less than accurate, which occurred of course to a minor degree. He couldn't have buried it north, even if he hadn't been worried about glaciation. If he'd buried it in Russia, it wouldn't have been a secret. Same for Canada and the United States. China was out of the question—Russia was fighting a land war with China and all across Europe with what remained of NATO.

"Africa or South America were the logical choices. But again, finding it might be difficult and getting it in and eventually getting it out could have proven a pretty rugged situation.

"But he was familiar with North Africa," Rourke went on, "from his work with terrorists. He had the most accurate geographic data available on Egypt from the days when the Egyptians had courted the Soviets and so on. And, Egypt afforded something that no other location possessed. The Great Pyramid. Thousands of tons, it wasn't about to be blown away. It would have taken eons, not centuries, for sand to cover it or wear it down. It wouldn't burn if the skies caught fire. It's about the most permanent thing on earth, really. And, he could get the tank of gas pretty

173

close to where he wanted to put it without taking the cannister from the vessel in which it was already berthed. The Suez Canal. Regular sky cranes were probably used to transport it and conventional earth moving equipment, or maybe some skillful demolitions, dug the hole. And, he had the ancillary advantage that if the cannister sprung a leak, who would know about it except the people he had working on the project, and he could have them eliminated if it came to that. Probably did have them eliminated anyway. There was a great tradition for that in the desert. The ones who buried the Pharoah were killed by the priests and the priests had their tongues cut out so they couldn't talk. Karamatsov probably carried that philosophy a step further—had his Elite Corps personnel kill the ones who killed the workers.

"But," Rourke sighed, studying the tip of his cigar, then looking at Michael, then from Michael to Captain Hartman, "that doesn't bring us any closer to what we really need to know, even if I'm anywhere close to being correct. Because we don't know the nature of the gas, assuming it is a gas, and so we don't know how to guard against it if it can be guarded against. But I'd opt for gas—if he uses it against the Underground City as it appears he intends, a gas will dissipate, become harmless after a time. A bacteria that could have survived five centuries might not be so easily neutralized."

"What do we do, then?"

"We go inside Karamatsov's camp and find out."

"Aww shit," Michael said, almost under his breath.

John Rourke laughed. "Your mother hates it when you swear—she always blames me."

Chapter Twenty-five

Portable radar units were positioned in the rocks surrounding the dry river bed in which they encamped, the vehicles camouflaged against casual aerial observation beneath a portion of the canyon wall which jutted angularly toward the gray late afternoon sky. The helicopters from the advance base in Norway were due in soon to the area, and Hammerschmidt's men just arrived, and with them Fraulein Doctor Maria Leuden. John Rourke noticed how she looked at his son.

Natalia had produced statistics—estimated troop strengths, numbers of vehicles and also photographs made by something like the Polaroid process, instantly developed, the camera part of the gear they had taken along for their mission of intelligence gathering which had so suddenly turned into a mission of warfare.

"For some reason, those greenhouses are important to Vladimir—I just have the feeling, John," she concluded.

Rourke took up his knife from beside him and handed it to Natalia. "Draw it out for me—it'll show us better than the pictures if we see it from your perspective."

Natalia began to scratch with Rourke's Gerber in

175

the dirt there that formed the floor of the overhang, the stark whiteness of fingers of drifted snow almost seeming to make the soil appear as dark as a blackboard. "The tunnel leading into the Underground City is here and to the right of it, when viewed from where we were, is the airfield. Vladmir's positions are about here. And the second element is positioned here, directly opposite the entrance. But the third element extends at a bizarre angle, its furthest reach putting it in jeopardy from the defenses, but it approaches these rectangles—the greenhouses."

John Rourke closed his eyes.

He listened as Hammerschmidt spoke. "Could there be, perhaps, some entrance underground from the greenhouses to the Underground City? Perhaps a service tunnel for electricity and water."

"It might be the only logical conclusion, Herr Doctor," Hartman added.

Lieutenant Milton Schmidt's voice: "Perhaps there is something, Herr Doctor Rourke, that exists in the greenhouses which is vital to the Marshal Karamatsov and he has extended his offensive line deliberately in order to facilitate a small group of commandoes reaching the greenhouses with minimum losses."

John Rourke opened his eyes.

Michael spoke. "Perhaps everyone is right. Perhaps there is some sort of access tunnel, perhaps not. But if it isn't a tunnel, perhaps there is a ventilator shaft or something. What if Karamatsov plans to somehow utilize the contents of that huge cylinder—assuming the contents to be a gas—by means of something in those greenhouses?"

John Rourke exhaled a thin gray stream of tobacco smoke and looked at his son, smiling. "You're a very clever fellow."

"Much as is his father," Natalia laughed.

John Rourke looked at her and grinned.

"To quote Michael, 'Perhaps everyone is right.' Even Michael. If Karamatsov has gas, he needs to use it. Can't flush it down the tunnel and hope it drifts inside. And what if some of his own people get killed in the process or incapacitated at least? The gas is useless unless he can employ it. Let's suppose that Karamatsov runs true to form—one plan backing up another." Rourke looked at Hammerschmidt. "When you and Michael insinuated yourselves into the group of technicians, then were forced to steal the truck after you were found out, he wasn't able to stop the truck until you guys were almost right at the Underground City's front door. He couldn't have planned on your doing that. And, like as not, you tipped his hand long before he was ready. And, you probably blew his scenario for using the gas—his primary scenario. Hypothetical question—let's say you have this gas and want to use it against the enemy but it's so dangerous you don't want to be anywhere near it; how do you do it?"

"Herr Doctor?"

"Lieutenant Schmidt—please sir."

"I would, I believe, infiltrate my agents, place cannisters of the gas in strategic locations and utilize radio detonation, or timers, to disperse the gas."

Rourke smiled at the young officer. "So would I. So would Karamatsov. Michael and your captain inadvertently prohibited him from doing so. He now falls back to plan B. That's the way the good marshal thinks."

"If there is a ventilation system or something similar," Natalia began.

"Then he would need to send a group of commandoes forward from the farthest forward point of his third line, and the third line would be close enough to

177

provide a heavy volume of covering fire, and—"

"And," Rourke interrupted Hammerschmidt, "he would achieve his intended original result. Get the gas released into the Underground City."

"We could send in a team of our own people," Natalia said, as if to herself, Rourke watching her. "If we could infiltrate without them knowing it, be waiting to intercept their personnel—then." She looked up. "Or am I missing the strategic objective?"

Hammerschmidt cleared his throat. "Fraulein Major—militarily, it might seem advisable for us to avoid interference with Marshal Karamatsov's plan. We fight the Soviet Union. If he destroys the occupants of its capital, its nerve center, he might inadvertently be assisting in the achievement of our final goal."

"Most of the people inside the Underground City, Otto are going to be women and children and old people. A lot of soldiers, sure—but a lot of innocent civilians, people who really haven't done anything to us. A question—because of the totalitarian leadership at the Complex, would it have been fair to the German people to destroy everyone inside the Complex just to get at the leadership?"

"This is a different question, Michael," Hammerschmidt responded, then stopped himself. He shook his head, "but perhaps it is not a different question."

For the first time, Maria Leuden, the archeologist, spoke. "Throughout history, warfare has taken huge numbers of non-combatant lives. In World War III, almost the entire population of earth was eradicated as a direct result of the bombing. The question, I think, is should we continue such a policy, or should we say that even if for no other reason than the vastly reduced numbers of our species, each life has value? I have no knowledge of how to win battles—perhaps I have spoken out of turn."

Rourke glanced from the woman to his son.

Rourke closed his eyes. "Those women and children and old people—they're the relatives of Karamatsov's soldiers outside the Underground City. Knowing the marshal, he probably has some sort of Elite Unit that will obey him no matter what. But no soldier is going to stand by while his commanding officer gasses his family to death. They may be holding the offensive lines, ready to attack because he's convinced them they will liberate their families, or propel the Soviet people to greatness or whatever. But he hasn't told them the gas will kill—if we're right and it is a gas and a lethal one. If we can get proof of what it will do, how would it be if a ranking officer of the KGB, the one-time wife of the marshal, were to inform the Russians at the barricades on both sides that Karamatsov was using them? Hmm?" Rourke opened his eyes.

Natalia smiled—and John Rourke realized the ineffectiveness of any defense he could muster against the blueness of her eyes.

Hammerschmidt declared, "It is worth a try, I think. Yes?"

"Yes," Rourke almost whispered.

Chapter Twenty-six

John Rourke extended his hands outward, palms upward.

Jea spoke, but as Rourke watched the eyes of Jea's people in the firelight, he could see that few understood more than a fraction of Jea's words.

Natalia spoke, trying to explain.

The eyes of the man called Char whom Rourke had fought, alternated from Natalia's body to the rifle—Soviet—which Jea had slung across his body, hanging beneath his right arm. Rourke had not had time to teach the boy to use the weapon, but no one in the tribal camp would know that, he theorized.

Natalia turned to John Rourke, shadows from the firelight flickering across her face, her eyes masked in darkness. "I told them as best I could. But so few of them understand."

"Ask Jea if he's ready."

Natalia nodded.

Rourke listened as Natalia spoke with Jea, watched the boy's face. There was no answering nod.

Instead, Jea removed the sling from his body and handed the rifle to Natalia—she took it from him as though accepting a gift.

Jea looked once at Rourke.

Rourke gave the young man a "thumbs up" sign—

there were grunts from the two dozen or so men, women and children of the tribe, as though this were some mystic symbol. Perhaps it was, Rourke mused.

Jea smiled, and then the smile faded as Jea turned to face Char and Rourke watched him in profile. Jea started forward, Char sensing the challenge, in Jea's body language, Rourke guessed, and Char looked at Rourke. Rourke touched at his own rifle, then let it fall to his side, shaking his head.

Char grinned toothlessly, then raised to his full height, his dirty looking, shaggy hair shaking, his fists bunching at the ends of his outstretched arms, then his elbows curling, his hands beating his chest like some sort of great ape or perhaps there was some racial memory of the fictional Tarzan.

Jea stopped less than two yards from the vastly larger, vastly stronger-seeming Char.

Jea's eyes—Rourke followed them as Jea stared suddenly left. On the ground at the far edge of the firelight lay an old man, dead.

Jea screamed, "Joe."

It was a scream beyond humanness.

Jea hurtled his body toward Char, Char's right fist hammering outward and downward, impacting Jea at the junction of the neck to the left shoulder, but Jea's right knee smashing up into the groin, Char bellowing, grasping Jea, falling, both men impacting the ground, rolling toward the fire, through the fire, the momentary smell of burning flesh, a scream from Jea, his woven bark covering aflame. Char kicked him as Jea rose, Jea falling back, into the dirt and snow, rolling as Char made to kick him again, the flames gone from Jea's clothing. Char threw himself half on top of the slighter man, Jea rolling away, his right arm and right leg pinned. Jea's left hand punched inward, toward Char's right ear, Char backhanding Jea across

181

the mouth with his own right, Jea's left arm flailing inward again, this time grabbing at the ear, ripping part of the shell of the ear away, blood spraying into the fire, the fire hissing with it, Char rolling back.

Jea was up, limping, his right arm hanging uselessly at his side. Char was to his knees, to his feet— Char reached to the fire, picking up into his five-pound ham-sized hands an enormous burning log, the diameter at least eight inches, the length at least three feet. He started forward, Jea limping back.

John Rourke swung the M-16 up to hip level, moving the selector to full auto and fired a long, ragged burst, severing the log a few inches above Char's upraised arms, burning embers falling into Char's hair and to his clothes, the big man screaming with rage.

Jea lunged for him, Jea's left shoulder impacting with Char's chest, the still upraised arms of the larger man leaving him wide open, Char falling back.

Jea was on him, dragging his right arm into action with his left, bunching both fists together, slamming them downward and across Char's face, then back, then across, then back again, Char's head twisting right and left and right and left again, the lips cracked, blood spurting from them. Char's hands grasped for Jea's throat, Jea still hammering away with both fists, hammering, the hands at Jea's throat going limp, the fingers dragging across Jea's flesh, clawing for it, the arms flailing, Jea's fists hammering the head and hammering at it.

Natalia's voice—"Jea. Jea!"

Jea's arms fell limp at his sides, his head lolling forward to his chest, his hands covered with Char's blood.

Char's face was unrecognizable as human . . .

The fingers, many of the bones in both hands, some

182

of the smaller bones in the wrists were broken. But Char was dead.

"This young man's going to Iceland whether he knows it or not—maybe as far as Argentina. He's going to need more than can be done for him in the field. Tell him, Natalia, that he was very brave, that we mourn for the loss of his father, that he will be a good leader for his people—and that we hope he never has to kill again."

Natalia was cleansing the wounds on Jea's face. "I think I know what I can do, John."

"I understand," John Rourke whispered to her.

And then Natalia began to speak with Jea as Rourke found a suitable injection that would leave Jea conscious but ease the pain in his smashed bones.

Chapter Twenty-seven

Paul and Annie had arrived by the time John Rourke, Natalia, the injured Jea, and six of Jea's tribe reached the rendezvous point. Hammerschmidt had briefed the new arrivals. By the face of Rourke's Rolex, it was eight P.M. Common Time and forward observers had indicated that the left flank of Karamatsov's forces was engaging the entrance to the Underground City.

Some of the climate controlled tents were already up and Rourke, Paul Rubenstein, and Michael Rourke and Otto Hammerschmidt had already begun to change.

One thing had not changed in five centuries—the Germans had military attire for every occasion.

Rourke began to strip out of his winter gear as he talked. "Two greenhouses are standing, the others destroyed. We'll split up, Captain Hammerschmidt, Michael—the two of you will take one, Paul and I will take the other." He was down to his underpants—and the experience reminded him he needed a shower, but there was no time and there were no readily available facilities. He took up the two piece black insulated long underwear, the legs of the underpants more like tights, no foot openings. One of the first places that long underwear failed during strenuous activity in the

184

field was where the legs stopped and the socks began, the two forever seeming to split apart. The Germans had planned around that. He sat in one of the folding chairs in order to skin into the pants. "As soon as we identify the cannisters, we eliminate Karamatsov's people before the gas can be put into use."

"What if you guys have guessed wrong?" Paul asked, trying to get into his underwear, and like all three other men doing it less than gracefully.

"We're up the proverbial creek," Rourke answered good naturedly. He stood, pulling up the underpants.

"Ballet anyone?" Hammerschmidt asked.

Rourke laughed aloud. "Thanks, but I was never much of a dancer." Rourke picked up the upper half of the undergarment, pulling it on over his head, long sleeved, crew necked. He started into the thin, insulated black coverall, the coverall of a stretchy material he learned as he began securing the fasteners to close it. He took to the chair again to secure the boots. Unlike the underwear and the jumpsuits, these were not sized in four general sizes, and were of a synthetic. He had been fitted for them before leaving Hekla. They were as form-fitting to the ankle as combat boots but were soled with something like rubber and rose to mid-calf height. They were ridiculously comfortable and thinly insulated.

He slipped the double Alessi rig across his shoulders like a vest. "This stuff gonna be warm enough?" Michael asked.

Hammerschmidt answered. "Our personnel have designed it, Michael, to withstand a temperature range from a cool evening in the desert to a cool morning in Antarctica—not a cold morning, but a cool one."

John Rourke buckled on his gunbelt with the Python in the full flap holster at his right side and the

Gerber MkII fighting knife at his left side. He watched as Michael attached the short sword-sized survival knife that seemed to be Michael's constant companion since leaving Hekla to the integral equipment harnessed jumpsuit, over the left lung.

Rourke secured the little A.G. Russell Sting IA Black Chrome which he usually carried inside the waistband of his Levis instead into the top of his left boot on the inside of the leg.

Hammerschmidt spoke again. "These utilities are designed not only for warmth and mobility, as you know. They are effective against skin contact with state-of-the-art gas warfare as best our scientists were able to determine."

John Rourke smiled as he unbagged his gas mask—black—and began checking the filter. It seemed a more sophisticated version of the regulation G.I. issue gas mask he had used five centuries earlier. He has such masks at the Retreat in their basic form. But the flanges of this mask were designed to be used in conjunction with a hood which tightly but comfortably covered the face, head and neck where the mask itself did not extend. As he reclosed the filter capsule, Rourke mused aloud, "What if what Karamatsov has is beyond 'state-of-the-art', Captain?"

Hammerschmidt said nothing for a moment, then pulled the toque-like hood over his head. As his eyes and nose and mouth re-emerged, he was smiling, "Then we are dead."

"Or," Paul added, laughing, "the situation has at least gotten serious."

John Rourke just looked at the younger man, then pulled his own hood in place. He adjusted it over his ears. Built into the hood was an earpiece which he fitted to his ear. Built into the gas mask was a radio microphone. He could communicate via this means with all members of the team or, within a given radius, with a position well behind friendly lines.

Paul pulled on his hood, adjusting it as Rourke had while Rourke watched.

Rourke picked up his M-16, giving it a quick visual and tactile going over, checking the seating of the thirty-round magazine, checking the tape applied to all points where the sling hardware could scrape and cause telltale noise. Hammerschmidt was securing the modern German version of a submachinegun to his chest—Uzi-like in appearance, though somewhat longer, it utilized the same caseless ammo as the German issue pistol. Rourke made a mental note to experiment with these new arms when time allowed, though he had no intention of modernizing his own armament since aside from the gadgetry aspects of the new Soviet and German weapons, they seemed no way improved over his own. Hammerschmidt was already into his pack—Rourke started into his.

Vestlike, the pack secured to the built in harness segments of the upper portion of the jumpsuit. As Michael started into his, Michael apparently realized he had positioned the knife incompatibly and was forced to remove it. Rourke tugged his shoulder holsters through the wide armholes of the vestlike battle pack, the holsters free, his pistols accessible.

He secured the extraction harness built into the vest between his legs, the extraction harness built sound-proof.

"What's the vest made of—Kevlar?"

Hammerschmidt turned to Paul Rubenstein, saying, "I am familiar with the term—but no, this is an advanced material, but I believe the functional principles are the same. The jumpsuit is of the same material as well. I am afraid neither the suit nor the vest will stop a rifle bullet, although the suit in combination with the vest will considerably reduce the effect."

The vest contained pouches built for the thirty-round magazines of the German submachineguns, two magazines riding in tandem per pouch. But by removing the separator, it accommodated the curved shape of the thirty-round Colt magazine satisfactorily. He loaded the pouches of the vest, watching as Michael did the same, then as Michael attached his huge knife to the vest. Rourke liked the look of the blade, the evident strength of the steel.

There was a holster built into the vest, for crossdraw carry and Rourke put one of the Detonics Scoremaster .45s into it, no room for the matching Scoremaster except into his pistol belt, between the belt and jumpsuit. He placed the second pistol there.

He looked about the tent.

Paul Rubenstein smiled, saying, "I feel like a man from Mars."

"Alpha Centauri, maybe—but not Mars," Rourke grinned back.

"I'm ready," Michael announced.

"As am I," Hammerschmidt said.

John Rourke picked up his rifle and his gloves. "Let's do it."

Chapter Twenty-eight

Natalia Anastasia Tiemerovna told Annie, "Sometimes, it's very distressing to be a woman."

It was dark in the climate controlled tent, dark except for the glow from the electronic panel which served to control temperature, ventilation, and humidity, dark except for the lantern which burned at the center of the table on which Natalia rested her booted feet.

Annie was seated to her right at the small table, crocheting, Natalia assumed, by feel. "We should be with them. If Momma were here, she'd want to be with them too."

"This is very uncomfortable for me."

"Me too—but more so for you, I guess."

"John was worried that if something went wrong—"

"Daddy loves you. He doesn't want Karamatsov getting his hands on you again."

"This is important—more important than my life is."

"What are you going to do?"

"I don't know, Annie." The door opened on the inside of the airlock and Natalia looked up, her hands going to the full flap holsters at her hips—but it was Maria Leuden. "Doctor Leuden—come and join us,"

189

Natalia offered.

"Thank you, Major Tiemerovna—I will."

"My name is Natalia."

"Call me Maria, please."

Annie giggled, "Well, Maria Please, it's nice to see you."

Maria Leuden laughed as she sat down opposite Natalia, Natalia swinging her feet back down to the floor. "I was worried about Michael—and your husband, Mrs. Rubenstein, the Herr Doctor and Otto Hammerschmidt."

"Annie—everybody calls me Annie. Even my mother's started to finally. Used to always call me Ann."

"Ann is a pretty name. It was my mother's name."

Natalia had never known her mother, except through those last reminiscences of her uncle, and her uncle had not really been her uncle. She envied people who knew their mothers' laughter, tears. "We were just saying that we didn't like being left behind," Natalia said, lighting one of the German cigarettes with her lighter. She exhaled a stream of smoke which settled about the lamp for a moment, then dissipated upward into the darkness—the cigarettes tasted terrible by comparison to the ones she remembered. She thought of the old saying, "Any port in a storm"—but she hadn't been that for John Rourke.

"I wouldn't know what to do," Maria Leuden said. "I mean—well, I have never been in combat—I—"

"It's not a heck of a lot of fun, Maria—let me tell you," Annie volunteered.

"It's different for the two of you—I mean—"

"A Russian major?"

"Yes, yes—Natalia. But—"

Annie set down her crocheting. "My husband, my father, and my brother are out there—along with a

German Army officer who seems like an all right guy. I'd like to be out there too, to keep them out of trouble."

Natalia started to speak, but didn't . . .

The most dangerous part was coming down the rock wall silently—John Rourke and Otto Hammerschmidt rapelled in tandem, Rourke's ears pricked for the slightest sounds—and there were many. Small rocks dislodged, in the otherwise almost unnatural stillness of the night, sounding like avalanches.

They kept going, the rapelling gloves Rourke wore easing along the rope as he worked it through the straight eight at the level of his abdomen. Beneath the special German rapelling gloves were the gloves that accompanied the jumpsuit, designed to seal with the wrists of the jumpsuit, specifically designed to guard against barbed wire and other potential sources of puncture.

He could see the ground beneath them clearly, see the roving team of guards, nearly at their maximum distance from the point at which Rourke had chosen that he and the others rapel. In a moment, the guards would be turning around, would start back, would be alerted.

Rourke pushed off again and jumped, breaking his fall against the harness, dropping into a crouch beside the rock wall, Hammerschmidt to the ground a second later. Rourke tugged at his rope three times, reaching to one of the leg pouches, opening the silent fastener.

His disliked using gimmicky weapons—but under the circumstances there was little choice.

Michael and Paul would be coming down quickly,

would be spotted by the guards.

Rourke palmed the blackened, forged stainless steel four-point Ninja star, another peculiar item utilized by the German commandoes.

He glanced toward Hammerschmidt—Hammerschmidt was ready.

They were blackness in blackness, the sky mercifully heavily overcast, their clothes designed to be like shadows in the night.

Rourke tugged away the rapelling glove, the sensitivity of the suit's gloves so excellent he could have operated while wearing them.

He spoke into the microphone in the face of his gas mask. "I've got the one on the right—at the count of three. One. Two. Three!"

Rourke hurtled the star, his target less than thirty feet away, already looking up along the face of the rock wall, apparently having heard Michael and Paul. The star buried itself in the throat of the man, a gurgling sound as Rourke dove forward, the second man going down as Rourke brought down the first, Rourke's knife in his right fist by the time he reached the body, but no need to use it, the man beneath him dead.

Rourke glanced toward Hammerschmidt—Hammerschmidt nodded back, Rourke hearing the voice in his ear, "Dead."

"Good—drag them this way," and Rourke grabbed the dead man by the ankles, hauling the body into the deeper shadow by the immediate base of the wall, withdrawing the shuriken only then, wiping it clean of blood on the dead man's uniform, returning the star to the pouch on the leg of his jumpsuit.

Immediately, he took up the man's rifle, removed the magazine, worked the action and popped the chambered round.

Quickly, Rourke searched the body—a utility folding knife, what apparently was Underground City currency, a handkerchief. No other weapons.

He field stripped the rifle, withdrawing the bolt, clutching it in his left fist as he ran toward the spot where Michael and Paul were finishing their descent. Rourke discarded the bolt into the darkness, putting it on the ground rather than throwing it. Michael was shucking the rope, Paul doing the same, each of them tugging at the ropes, the ropes being drawn up by Hammerschmidt's men under the command of Sergeant Dekker.

The rear of the Soviet position nearest to the greenhouses was some two hundred yards away. Paul was helping with Rourke's rifle, the rifle secured to the rear of the harness for the descent. As soon as the rifle was clear, Paul said, "Get me."

"Right," and Rourke turned around, Paul with his back to him, Rourke undoing the lashings for the Schmiesser Paul had secured there. Michael and Otto Hammerschmidt were doing the same for each other.

Rourke said two words into the microphone in his mask. "No guns." And with his unburdened left hand, he signalled that they move out, breaking into a long strided loping run. He remembered a line from the many adventures of Sherlock Holmes—"The game is afoot!"

Chapter Twenty-nine

They had agreed it would be knives and hands and garrotes, but guns would not be used, unless it meant the sacrifice of the entire team.

John Rourke ran at the lead, to his right Paul Rubenstein, behind them Michael and Otto Hammerschmidt, in Rourke's right fist the black catspaw-handled Gerber MkII, his rapelling gloves stashed in the large leg pocket on the left leg of the jumpsuit, the lens material of the gas masks surprisingly insusceptible to fogging during exertion and the mask itself surprisingly comfortable to wear.

They hugged the rock wall until its end, having crossed half the length of the rear of Karamatsov's line. At the edge of the rock wall they stopped, Rourke speaking into the built-in microphone. "Son-of-a-bitch is pretty confident—so far. Hope he stays confident and doesn't expect anything from his rear. Follow my lead—let's go," and Rourke started ahead again.

He suddenly found himself smiling, wondering if he would ever get too old for this. His son was thirty, his daughter twenty-eight. Biologically, he would have had to have fathered them before he was ten except for the manipulation of the cryogenic chambers.

He would have been a grandfather in a matter of months—if it hadn't been for Vladmir Karamatsov killing his daughter-in-law, Madison.

As he ran, he tried recalling if he had ever really hated before.

John Rourke admitted to himself that he loved Natalia, and the facile answers he had given Michael, his son, were not complete answers. But Sarah was his wife and he loved Natalia no more than Sarah—but he realized too that he loved her no less.

One of the Soviet jeep-like vehicles, Rourke speaking into his mask, "Otto—Michael—go get 'em," and he dodged left, Paul running even beside him now, at the far right corner of his restricted peripheral vision—restricted because of the mask—seeing Michael as if in slow motion, Michael's right gloved fist moving to his chest, withdrawing the massive life Support System II, as Michael had called it. Michael had asked if he—Rourke—had known Jack Crain and Rourke had told his son yes, the Texas knifemaker a valued friend and one of the unrivalled best at his craft. His design had stood the test of five centuries, unchanged. He hadn't told his son that he owned the five centuries before original that Crain had made for him. It was one of the few surprises still at the Retreat which neither Michael nor Annie had seen. He had saved it to give to Michael. But now he would use it.

Michael moved right, Hammerschmidt left, toward the targets of the two men who stood beside the Soviet vehicle, the two—Michael and Hammerschmidt—moving as though in some ballet, working remarkably well together. There was a sixth sense that men who fought together and routinely saved each other's lives developed. He and Paul had this. It seemed that somehow Michael and Otto Hammerschmidt had it as well.

To the left, Hammerschmidt struck, his target wheeling toward him, raising his Soviet Animov-60 assault rifle, Hammerschmidt knocking the weapon aside as he plunged the blade into the throat with a rapier thrust, withdrawing, hacking with the German bayonet across the side of the neck, a spray of blood in the halflight.

Michael—his man had turned abruptly, Michael visibly wrenching his body out of the run into a classic martial arts pose, the left knee coming up, the body seeming to relax, the left leg pistoning down, the right leg snapping upward and outward, catching the Soviet assault rifle at the small of the stock, the rifle flying skyward, Michael twisting his body, rolling, catching the rifle, then tossing it to Hammerschmidt.

The Soviet soldier edged back along the ground, Michael going for him, the flash of a blade—Rourke couldn't tell the type at the distance. Rourke made to start toward them, felt Paul's hand restraining him at his left forearm. But Michael was moving, the massive Life Support knife in both fists bisecting the line of Michael's left upper arm, the knife point downward. As the Soviet soldier charged, Michael sidestepped right, pivoting on his left foot, the knife in Michael's hands seeming almost to have a deadly will of its own, Michael's arms swinging like a baseball player in the batter's box, the blade of the knife hacking through the left side of the Soviet soldier's neck, the body freezing in stop-motion, spinning out slowly, falling, Michael pivoting again on his left foot, his right leg going out to almost maximum extension as the knife in his hands raised high overhead then chopped downward, the Soviet soldier's helmet splitting into two perfectly even halves, another spray of blood as the knife contacted the skull.

The body fell.

John Rourke could hear Paul Rubenstein's voice in his earpiece. "Quite a boy, isn't he?" And then Paul laughed.

Rourke started running again, glancing back once—Michael and Otto Hammerschmidt were behind them, the Soviet assault rifles in their hands.

To the right, from the front of Karamatsov's lines, there was gunfire, and from the far right, by the airfield hundreds of yards away, there was the boom of artillery and the night sky was nearly as bright as day for an instant.

Artillery answered almost immediately from near the entrance to the Underground City, more flashes of light, a strange electronic noise of a level that made the ears ring. "The energy weapons—artillery," Hammerschmidt's voice said, coming through the earpiece.

"Shit—if Karamatsov's attacking, we might be too late!" Rourke waved the others foward, breaking into a dead run now, artillery shells exploding around them on all sides, the energy weapons seeming to cause the earth to ripple as things like lightning bolts impacted the ground.

Rourke dodged left, angling toward the furthest extension of Karamatsov's lines that approached the greenhouses. There was a flash of brilliant light as another of the energy weapons fired, huge machines the size of field artillery—but in the flash of light, John Rourke could see the shadow of a figure, then another and perhaps more, running toward the greenhouses.

Soviet troops ran about everywhere—mortar teams

setting up, riflemen withdrawing from positions under heavy artillery and mortar fire from the tunnel entrance to the Underground City.

A Soviet trooper passed within two yards of John Rourke, running—he never stopped.

They were nearing the furthest extension of the battle line now, the greenhouses more clearly visible. The M-16 in Rourke's right fist, his arm extended, he worked the selector to auto—a phalanx of Soviet soldiers suddenly throwing themselves up like a wall across Rourke's path. Rourke fired, the M-16 bucking in his fist, the flatter sound of Soviet assault rifles behind him—Michael's voice through Rourke's earpiece, "It's me—me and Hammerschmidt!"

The sharp crack of a three-round burst from Paul's submachinegun—silence didn't matter now, the sounds of battle enveloping them.

John Rourke closed with the line of Soviet troopers, emptying the M-16, then snapping the front handguard against his left palm, ripping the butt of the rifle forward and into a Soviet face, kicking the body away with his left foot, whirling right, smashing the flash deflector of the M-16 diagonally across the bridge of the nose of another Soviet trooper, Rourke's right foot snapping up and out, catching the man in the groin.

Rourke jumped over the body as it sagged downward, glancing behind him, Paul emptying his Schmiesser into one man, using the butt of the weapon like a cudgel against the face of another, then running again.

Rourke couldn't see Michael or Hammerschmidt—but then he heard Michael's voice in his earpiece, "We're on the way!"

Rourke said nothing, changing sticks in the M-16

as he ran, putting the empty into the pouch on his vest just vacated, running, working the charging handle and stripping the top round off the fresh thirty-pound magazine.

Two Soviet troopers with Animov rifles running to cut him off—he fired, one three-round burst, then another, cutting both men down.

At the far left edge of his peripheral vision, Rourke could see Paul, saying into his microphone to the younger man, "Paul—the furthest greenhouse out—go for it!"

"Right!"

Rourke stopped, wheeled a full one hundred eight degrees and sprayed the M-16 into the Soviet troops starting for them, hosing them down, bodies jackknifing into the darkness, illuminated then for an instant in another flash of artillery fire, then disappearing.

The M-16 empty, Rourke let it drop to his side on its sling, his left fist snatching the Scoremaster from his belt, his right going for the Scoremaster in the vest's built-in holster.

His thumbs jacked back the hammers, his first fingers twitching the triggers. Single shots—he couldn't afford the luxury of double taps—men going down as he fired. He started to run, almost at the edge of the line now, mortar plates here, tubes belching gray smoke against the darkness, machinegun nests firing maddeningly, Paul's voice, "Barbed wire—watch it, John—I'm over."

Rourke acknowledged, "Thanks—Michael—Hammerschmidt—you catch that?"

"Got it."

Ahead of him now, both pistols nearly empty, Rourke could see the wire, concertina—how little some things had changed, he thought fleetingly.

A Soviet trooper lunged for him, Rourke emptying the last round in each pistol into the trooper's chest, Rourke's arms going out, grasping for the body as it sagged away, launching the body over the concertina wire, the wire depressing under the weight, Rourke leaping up, vaulting over the wire across the dead man's back.

He was clear of the wire, ramming both pistols into his gunbelt, the slides still locked open and empty. The M-16—he found it with his right fist, grabbing another magazine, ramming it up the well, pouching the empty, running as he let the bolt slam home.

The furthest greenhouse was perhaps three hundred yards—he could see Paul ahead of him.

A lightning bolt pulse from an energy weapon impacted the ground near Rourke's feet and Rourke felt the shock wave of the artillery fire, felt it slap him down, tucking his body into a roll as he fell, coming up out of it, to his knees, dirt and debris falling about him like rain.

To his feet, he lurched forward, his body still rocking with the impact—he ran on.

Two hundred yards to go, Paul well ahead of him now, almost to the greenhouse's near wall, in the flash of light from a conventional artillery burst Paul silhouetted against the wall for an instant.

Rourke looked back—Michael, clearing the fence in a running jump using a body as his platform, Hammerschmidt right behind him, a Soviet assault rifle in each of the German commando's hands.

A hundred yards, the artillery—conventional and energy—increasing in intensity, but here in the no-man's land between the battle lines, the chance of impact from artillery or mortar fire more remote.

Rourke could see Paul vanish into the greenhouse,

Rourke throwing himself into the run, safing the rifle, the M-16 dropping to his side, changing magazines for the Scoremasters from the musette bags that hung at either side of his gear, running the slides forward, working the ambidextrous safeties up, leaving the pistols cocked and locked, one in each fist.

He threw himself to the ground beside the greenhouse, catching his breath for an instant, trying to segregate sounds from within the greenhouse from those of the battle which raged behind him and in front of him.

He thought he heard the working of a slide—a silenced pistol?

To his feet, Hammerschmidt's voice in his ear. "We are entering the near greenhouse—we see them—four persons. One may be a woman. They have a cannister—"

Hammerschmidt's voice cut out as Rourke ran along the length of the greenhouse. He heard a burst of subgun fire—Paul.

There was a glass door, steel or some other metal reinforced—Rourke's left foot snapped forward as he wheeled half right, a double Tae-Kwon-Do kick to the glass, the glass shattering, Rourke stabbing both pistols into his belt, catching up the M-16, with the butt of the rifle knocking out the remainder of the glass, diving through as glass in one of the window panels near his left arm shattered. "Look out, John!" Paul's voice, heard in the earpiece and heard normally. Rourke looked to his right as he hit the floor of the greenhouse and rolled, assault rifle fire ripping the concrete block floor beside his head, Rourke squinting his eyes involuntarily against the dust spray despite the protection of the gas mask. As he came out of the roll he fired the M-16 toward the flash from the darkness. There was a scream—clearly a woman.

To his feet—and he heard Paul's whispered voice in his ear. "I'm to your left John—three of 'em left in here I think."

Rourke edged right, ducking behind a table where broad leafed plants—some of the leaves chewed partially away by gunfire—were racked. Water dribbled down along the length of the table, some of the plants overturned. He saw movement at the far end of the greenhouse.

He spoke into the microphone that was built into the mask. "Paul—move up along the left. I'll move up along the right—before you shoot—"

"I know—you do the same."

Rourke reached to the M-16, his right fist closing on the pistol grip. In a crouch, he started forward, between the tables of plants and the greenhouse wall, picking his footing carefully, hoses, pipes, shattered pots from plants, fallen trays of seedlings everywhere.

When the first of them had entered the greenhouses, Natalia would have been put on alert, the helicopter waiting for her. But it would do no good for her to appeal to the Soviet combatants if Rourke or Paul or Michael or Hammerschmidt didn't get the information on the gas that would give her the facts she needed to convince the fighters that Karamatsov was only using them.

Rourke spoke into his microphone, whispering lest his voice be heard by his adversaries ahead somewhere in the darkness at the far end of the greenhouse. "Natalia—you hear me?"

The voice was weaker because of her location well behind the lines. "I hear you, John—you and Paul—and Michael and the captain—"

"We're fine. As soon as we get to the gas—be

ready."

"Be careful—I love you always."

Rourke closed his eyes for an instant. "God help me—I love you—be ready," and he continued moving, the M-16 held tight against his chest, not the ideal weapon for the confined space but his only weapon capable of a sufficient volume of fire.

"John—about thirty yards up—there's some sort of valve control—one of them is there—on your side."

Rourke squinted into the darkness—he could barely see the figure. He edged closer to the tables, slowly, silently, unslinging the M-16, not even resetting the safety tumbler lest the click be heard. Rourke reached to his left boot top, withdrawing the Russell Black Chrome Sting IA—he chose it over the Gerber because there was no snap built into the sheath, no snap to open and be heard.

His eyes focused tight to the ground, looking for shards of pottery or other objects which might be crushed by his body weight and make a betraying noise. The occasional close bursts of artillery or mortar fire and the muffled sounds of the more distant discharges and explosions would help, he knew.

He could see the figure clearly now, on guard it seemed, what appeared to be a silenced SMG in its hands, the muzzle wavering right to left—as long as the muzzle moved, the subgunner held no definite target, Rourke realized. Once it stopped moving, either he or Paul would be in trouble.

Rourke kept moving, hearing Michael's voice in his earpiece. "Dad—we got them, all of them. One of them—Hammerschmidt put a knife to the man's throat and the guy threw up and then he told us about the gas. It's something totally new—but you were

203

right, Karamatsov stashed it five centuries ago just after the Night of The War. It has a biological effect once it's inhaled—it's not skin absorptive, but it's colorless, odorless, and tasteless so no one will know it's being used until it's too late. It affects male hormones—triggers unbridled aggression. Karamatsov could have turned every man in the Underground City into a homicidal maniac."

Rourke didn't answer his son—to have used his voice would have betrayed his position. He had narrowed the distance to the subgunner to ten yards. With his left hand, his right clutching the Sting IA, he picked up a pottery fragment, hurtling it well ahead of Paul's estimated position on his left, the subgunner wheeling right, firing, Rourke to his feet in a dead run, hurtling his body against the subgunner—it was a woman. The impact of Rourke's body slammed the woman into the glass wall and through. Rourke's right hand thrusting forward, the knife cutting into her throat, the subgun still firing in her dead hands, shards of glass streaming around Rourke as Rourke pushed himself up and back, a massive piece of glass falling, impaling the woman through the throat.

Natalia's voice in his ear as Rourke drew back against the plant tables, still without his rifle, wiping the blood from his blade by stabbing it into the dirt of an overturned rubber plant. "John—are you all right?"

"Yeah—fine. You heard Michael?"

"I'm going to be airborne in less than a minute."

"Be persuasive—if you can't get them to lay down their arms, at least get them to withdraw from the field. We've got two more here to get."

Paul's voice. "John—I found 'em—hurry!"

Rourke was to his feet, resheathing the knife, no

time to go back and grab his rifle, no time to reach for the submachinegun in the hands of the dead Russian woman and search her for spare magazines. His fists found the butts on the Detonics Scoremaster .45s in his belt, ripping them free, thumbing down the safeties, running.

Assault rifle fire—the answering report of Paul's submachinegun. Rourke said into his microphone, "Michael—you and Hammerschmidt get out with the gas cannister—get it airborne to Argentina fast. That tank they dug up out of the desert would have held thousands of gallons of the stuff in liquid form— probably concentrated. That's the primary objective—get it out."

"Right—on the way—good luck."

Rourke reached the end of the long row of tables, the gunfire again, distinct, just ahead and to the left. He jumped onto the table to better see what was happening, the sound of a blower starting, Paul locked in combat hand-to-hand with a man at least a head taller, another man working the valves on a silver colored metallic cylinder attached to a pipe stem. Rourke thrust both pistols up to eye level and fired, then again and again and again, the body of the person beside the cannister rocking with the hits, spinning, falling. Rourke took a running leap, by-passing Paul and the man Paul fought, lunging for the cannister valves.

"Jesus—" The valves were wide open—he started turning them closed—but the valves, he realized, were threaded so the handle would slip off the stem after opening, so the valves could not be closed.

"Michael—Otto—don't work the cannister valves—they're one way valves. The cannister has to be bled into another container under controlled conditions."

"Understood."

Rourke wheeled—Paul's right fist was crossing the jaw of his opponent, the man falling back, the pistol sailing from his hand, his body lurching toward John Rourke. Rourke upped the safeties of his pistols and stabbed them into his belt, grabbing at the falling Russian, twisting the man around, Rourke's right fist finding one of the Scoremasters again.

He put the pistol to the man's half glazed right eye. "Can the cannister be closed, or the pipe cut off?"

The man laughed through his protective mask. Rourke laced the Scoremaster across the top of the man's head and let the body sag.

To his feet—Rourke cursed himself for not thinking of it a moment earlier. The blower. He reached the controls—the dials had been twisted off. Pliers—he needed pliers—had no pliers. Wire cutters—no time. His eyes followed to the base of the blower unit—the power cable connecting it to the electrical output. "Paul—outa here—quick!"

Rourke stabbed the Scoremaster that was in his right fist toward a cable and fired, the 185-grain JHP severing the cable, sparks flying, then suddenly flames erupting from the machine in a loud whoosh. Rourke jumped back.

He upped the Scoremaster's safety and ran, back the way he had come, vaulting over the potting table, to the concrete block walkway, running as he rammed both pistols into his belt. "Paul—we've gotta get into the Underground City—see what can be done—see the effects of the gas. It's our only defense against it now."

Rourke passed the M-16 he had left behind, snatching it up, running still, Paul waiting beside the blown out portion of a wall for him, changing sticks in the MP-40 subgun.

Rourke reached the opening, both of them running now, Natalia's voice ringing through the air overhead from a lightless, soundless helicopter in the night sky. She spoke in Russian, her voice pleading, clear, emphatic. "Comrades—you have been betrayed—by my husband, Vladmir Karamatsov. He is not a hero, but a traitor, to you, to Russia, to all the people of the world, to Russia's history. He is unspeakably evil. He has you fighting, brother against brother, father against son—all to serve his own ends of power. He has used commando teams to reach the greenhouses between the front lines of the attacking forces and the entrance to the Underground City. The commando teams carried a deadly gas unlike any ever used before, even in the most vicious of fighting. It affects only men—it works with male sex hormones to acti-vate feelings of violent aggression deep within the brain, to turn every man inside the Underground City into a madman, blood-crazed, turning on his com-rades, male and female alike, to kill children, the old, the sick—just to kill. Fall back, Comrades—don't fight and die so Vladmir Karamatsov can make himself your dictator. Fall back, Comrades. This is Major Natalia Anastasia Tiemerovna of the Commit-tee for State Security—in the name of the Soviet people, fall back!"

John Rourke and Paul Rubenstein ran toward the tunnel entrance of the Underground City, the artillery fire slowing, howls of rage and madness filling the night air, and behind them, as Rourke wheeled to check their rear, Soviet troops from Karamatsov's command were running forward, their rifles not in assault positions, some of them without rifles at all, casting their helmets to the ground. A man was screaming the name of his wife, running with his arms outspread—a burst of automatic weapons fire from the barricades to the Underground City cut him down and he fell, his face slipping down into a shell hole.

Natalia's words again from the helicopter overhead over the loud hailing system—"Two men move among you—they are dressed all in black—but these men are not your enemies, but rather helped to prevent one of the cannisters of this deadly gas from being released into the ventilation system of the Underground City— they are your comrades. The second cannister was released—the gas does its evil work now. Men of Karamatsov's Legions—do not enter the Underground City even to save your families unless you wear gas masks. Women are safe to enter, but there is madness in the Underground City. This is Major Natalia Anastasia Tiemerovna of the Committee for State Security of the Soviet—"

And there was madness, men at the barricades fighting swarms of attackers streaming from the tunnel of the Underground City entrance.

Guns, knives, fists, rifle butts—Rourke hissed into his face mask microphone, "Paul, what was the diameter of that pipe do you think?"

"Two inches—maybe a little more—you're thinking—"

"With the airflow cut off, it'll take longer for that gas to filter through the pipe, won't it? What if we make it through the tunnel and block the pipe before it hits the ventilation system, or shut off the ventilation system entirely—let's do it!"

They were near the metallic defense shields now, soldiers at the barricades fighting enemies from behind them now, female defenders having the worst of

208

it, men from the Underground City still pouring from its bowels, attacking women as the women ran into the city to rescue loved ones.

Rourke clambered up onto the barricade, the screams of madness, the sporadic gunfire, the howls of pain everywhere around him. Two men fought, their eyes wide, their lips drawn back like animals, their teeth bared, in their hands knives—they were stabbing each other but still grappling, their bodies splashed with each other's blood. Rourke jumped from the barricade, seeing a blur of black against the metallic shields—Paul Rubenstein right beside him.

Rourke shoved past the dueling men, running, his assault rifle in his right fist tensioned tight against its sling, his eyes darting left and right.

A horde of men poured from the Underground City, their uniforms tinged with blood, madness in their eyes. A blond haired woman in full battle uniform except for her helmet which was nowhere in evidence—six of the men charged her and she backed away. "Paul!"

"Right!"

Rourke angled right, the M-16 falling to his side on its sling, his hands reaching out, grappling the nearest of the six men to the ground with a simple shoulder grip, his right foot going out behind the man's right knee, Rourke's right fist hammering outward, slamming into the man's jaw, the head snapping back. The blow would normally have put a man of average size down unless he were a boxer and his jaw toughened. The man was of average size—but instead he growled, rolled, drew a pistol from his belt and raised it to fire as Rourke sidestepped, drawing one of the Scoremasters, his thumb working down the safety, his first finger touching to the trigger, the Scoremaster bucking once in his hand, the center of the man's forehead suddenly splotched red with blood, the top of the head—because of the angle of the shot—erupting outward, blood oozing from the exit wound.

John Rourke didn't know if the gas induced condition were temporary or permanent—he had no desire to kill someone who was already a victim.

He wheeled right, Paul Rubenstein hammering down another of the men with the butt of his Schmiesser, swinging it like a battle hammer.

The blond haired girl—the other four men had cornered her, ringed her, were forcing her back against the tunnel wall.

She raised her rifle—but in her eyes, Rourke saw that she would not shoot until it was too late.

Rourke launched himself toward the four men, throwing his body in a body block against the backs of two of the men, throwing the men in turn into their comrades in madness, the four going down, Rourke rolling away, his wind gone for an instant.

To his feet—he lurched back, shaking his head to clear it, Paul Rubenstein stepping in, wrestling an Animov assault rifle away from one of the men, swinging it like a baseball bat, the stock splitting as rifle contacted jaw bone, the man's head snapping back.

Rourke shook his head again, taking two long steps forward, wheeling on his right foot, his left foot snapping up and out, a double kick to the chest of one man, his left foot swinging downward as his upper body pitched slightly, his right foot snapping up and out and back, into the chest of another of the men.

Rourke wheeled forward, his left fist snaking out, hooking the jaw of the man he had just kicked in the chest, hammering the man down. Paul was on the fourth man now, the battered Browning High Power in his right fist, the butt of it hammering into the skull of the fourth man.

Rourke wheeled a full 360 degrees, his assault rifle coming up, the Scoremaster he realized unconsciously shoved back into his belt—mechanically, with his left hand he felt for the safety. It was upped.

The Russian girl stared. "Who are—"

In Russian, he answered her back. "John Rourke. Paul here and myself—we couldn't prevent them using the second cannister. You can help us—help your people. The gas is coming from the greenhouse nearest to the barricades through a pipe maybe two inches in diameter. The pipe feeds to the ventilation system for the Underground City somehow. If we can block the pipe or close off the ventilation system, we can stop some of the gas, maybe as much as half of it. Help us."

The girl licked her lips. "Yes—come with me—hurry!"

She started into a run, almost seeming to spring along the length of the tunnel, Rourke telling Paul through the microphone, "Come on!"

"Right behind you, John."

Rourke threw himself into the run, his assault rifle in his right fist by the pistol grip, Paul at the edge of his peripheral vision, the Schmiesser in an assault position but held high.

Men, their hands dripping blood—three of them started for the blond haired Russian girl a few paces ahead of Rourke, Rourke stepping into them, blocking them, his rifle butt snapping up and out, Paul wheeling, kicking a second man in the crotch, then hammering the man to the floor of the tunnel with a blow from his Schmiesser across the back of the neck.

The third man drew a knife, lunging for the girl, Rourke snapping the rifle butt outward, missing the jaw, the man wheeling away from the girl, toward him. Rourke drew back, letting the rifle drop to his side on its sling. He drew the big Gerber MkII from his belt, telling the man, "I am your friend—put down the knife and I will try to help you. Believe me—" The man lunged, Rourke side-stepping. He was running out of time. John Rourke whispered, "God forgive me," and snapped his right arm out to full extension, the spearpoint of the fighting knife driving into the right side of the madman's neck just beneath the ear.

The blond haired woman looked at him. "Hurry," she almost whispered.

"Yes," Rourke nodded.

Paul was already running, a few yards ahead, the stream of madmen running along the tunnel not seeming to ebb, but Rourke realizing that apparently as the madness grew there was no selectivity, all was lost around the men—they killed each other.

Rourke dodged past a knot of the unfortunates, the end of the tunnel just ahead, a group of women there, fighting off a group of male attackers. Rourke angled toward them, the blond woman beside him, Paul Rubenstein turning toward them, Rourke throwing himself into the knot of attackers, rifle butting them down, his feet kicking them away as they tried to rise.

The Russian girl shouted to the other women. "These two men—they help us. We must reach the main ventilation system controls—if we must fight our way every step of the way, by the time we reach the controls it will do no good. Help us!"

One of the women, then another and another—they picked up rifles and knives from the unconscious men around them. One of the women—big, overly large in every proportion, her face plain, heavy glasses over her eyes, shouted, "Comrades! To battle!"

And the woman started to run, a wedge ahead of Rourke and Paul Rubenstein and the blond haired girl, the beefy looking woman using an inverted rifle like a club, swatting away attackers as they lunged for her or the others.

A man jumped from behind a stacked row of crates, a blood dripping knife in his right fist—Rourke chopped the flash deflector of the M-16 down and across the right side of the man's head, wheeling as he made the blow, putting the madman down.

They ran on, past the secondary barricade shields, most of them turned over. Fires raged within the cavern just beyond the tunnel, vehicles overturned, sporadic gunfire everywhere.

John Rourke understood the concept of Hell.

Men in the same uniforms attacked each other, beat each other mercilessly, their uniforms already blood drenched.

Karamatsov—"Mother fucker," Rourke hissed.

"What?"

It was Paul's voice.

"Karamatsov—I'll get him, so help me God."

They ran on, turning right down a small corridor, some of the women who had joined them falling back, one of the women, small by comparison to the blond girl, miniscule by comparison to the bulky woman, shouting, "It is this way—hurry!"

The big woman shouted, "Comrades—we shall hold them here—form a line! On me—hurry!"

Rourke glanced back at the woman—the big woman's eyes met with his. Behind the glasses the eyes were pretty and they smiled.

Rourke shouted at her, "We'll make it—Comrade!"

He threw himself into the run, nearly outdistancing the blond girl, turning a corridor left, then a right, massive double doors swung open, the ventilation room sprawling before them, as huge as the generator rooms he had seen in power plants, the ceiling a hundred feet high at least, steel catwalks and narrower girders lacing the airspace.

The small woman shouted, "It is down there—two levels down!"

The blond girl ran ahead—but on the catwalk as they started across toward the ladders leading downward were men in technician's coveralls, pistols in their hands, the look of madness in their eyes.

Rourke shoved past the blond, Paul Rubenstein shouldered in beside him, Paul shoving the small girl behind him.

Rourke's eyes and Paul's eyes met. "Shoot!" Rourke almost whispered into his microphone.

Rourke stabbed the M-16 forward, Paul the Schmeisser—both weapons opened up simultaneously ripping the technicians from the catwalk, hurtling them downward into the machinery six floors below.

Rourke ran ahead, reaching the ladder, looking for the controls two floors below—he could see a massive panel on an island of steel which formed the center of a wheel spoked with catwalks from four sides. "Is that it?" he shouted to the Russian woman.

"Yes—I think so," the blond called back.

The smaller girl shouted. "That is it—the master control is encased in plastic—a big red switch. My lover—he works here and sometimes—"

"Never mind—stay there—hold the catwalk—be careful."

Rourke reached to the parallel vertical runners, his gloved fists knotting over them, his feet against the

214

sides of the runners, tight—he let himself drop, skidding down the ladder as though it were a pole, swinging away as he reached the level below. No one. He looked up—Paul was coming but not as quickly.

Rourke reached to the ladder again, the woman a floor above fighting off two more technicians, finally the blond haired soldier using her assault rifle, the concrete and steel around them reverberating with the shots.

Rourke started down the ladder again, dropping, swinging inward to the larger catwalk which ringed the spokes and the hub at the center where the controls were.

He could see the plastic boxed red master control switch—but on the catwalk, between him and the controls, was a man, the man's size extraordinary. He was a soldier, his helmet gone somewhere, his rifle inverted like a club, his eyes wide with the madness.

John Rourke stepped out onto the catwalk, saying to the man, "I am here to help you and make you well. Put down your rifle—just step back. I need to reach the switch."

The man screamed, stood his ground.

Rourke started across, edging forward slowly, ready to use a gun, not wanting to.

"Please," Rourke whispered.

The big man—six foot six or better, over two hundred and fifty pounds—charged, swinging his assault rifle in huge circles over his head.

John Rourke eyed the man.

John Rourke eyed the switch.

Rourke drew both of the small Detonics pistols from beneath his arms, thumbing back the hammers.

The man still came, the madness in his eyes—

John Rourke fired a simultaneous double tap with

the twin stainless Detonics .45s, the massive man's body rocking, Rourke wanting to reach for him, the body falling back as Rourke stepped toward the man, the rifle falling over the catwalk, the huge man's body tumbling after it, a scream lingering on the air, a heavy slapping sound as the body stopped against the concrete four floors below.

Rourke closed his eyes for an instant—he opened his eyes and ran forward, toward the island, upping the safeties of the pistols in his hands, inverting them, smashing the butts of the pistols against the plastic protective covering, the plastic cracking, falling away as it shattered.

Rourke stuffed the pistol from his right fist into his belt—he jerked down the switch.

There had been a loud humming sound—and the humming sound stopped.

Chapter Thirty

It had taken three hours for the gas volume to diminish satisfactorily that the men whose minds the gas had affected—those who still survived—simply sat down and fell asleep.

With Paul Rubenstein, John Rourke had vanished from the Underground City, the German force still not strong enough to penetrate it and hold it.

Rourke had stopped for a moment—the large woman lay dead in the corridor where she had gone down fighting to buy Rourke, Rubenstein, and the two other women time in which to shut down the ventilation system.

Rourke had bent over her, closed her eyes, folded her glasses neatly beside her, then run on.

He had a camera, using it to photograph the Soviet defenses, Paul Rubenstein doing the same, both men feeling almost unclean somehow doing it.

There was a chance of peace, perhaps, with the survivors of the Underground City—a chance perhaps.

The small German force, with the aid of members of Jea's tribe, had performed two tasks: taking prisoners from among Karamatsov's forces for interrogation and prisoners from among those affected by the gas in order to study the gas's effects to be able to

217

defend against it.

The bulk of Karamatsov's force—more than eight thousand men and women and the majority of the still battleworthy equipment—had moved out to the east, German units following at a discreet distance to plan the next move in the growing war.

Several thousand of the Russians—men and women—had lain down their arms, going to aid their families and comrades within the Underground City. But those among the thousands in Karamatsov's force who had broken off from battle made up an estimated three-fifths of the total who had lain down their arms.

John Rourke considered it a sign that humanity still possessed a basic good—even after all that had befallen it.

John Rourke, Natalia Tiemerovna, Annie and Paul Rubenstein, Michael Rourke, Otto Hammerschmidt, Captain Hartman, and Fraulein Doctor Maria Leuden stood on the wall of rock overlooking the Underground City, vehicles still smoldering from artillery or mortar hits, the ground between the high rock wall and the entrance to the Underground City pockmarked with shell holes, blackened with fire, littered with dead.

John Rourke held Natalia's hand.

John Rourke spoke, his face turned into the wind, the sun bright, his eyes, despite the dark lensed aviator sunglasses, squinted against it. "Karamatsov will need a manufacturing base for re-supply. He'll have to avoid battle until he finds it. He'd have fuel and ammunition cached, but that won't last forever. If there's a civilization to the east, he'll find it, use it. We don't have the manpower to engage him now. But we have to go after him."

Annie asked, "What will we do?"

"Try to outthink his next move. If he headed east,

he headed east for a reason. We have to find out what. Before he gets there."

John Rourke cupped his hands around the battered Zippo windlighter, thrusting the tip of his cigar into the blue-yellow flame.

"Jea asked me something before he was airlifted to the hospital in Argentina," Natalia said softly.

"What did he say, Fraulein Major?" Hammerschmidt asked.

John Rourke looked at Natalia, Natalia's voice sounding strained, tired. "Jea asked—'Is fighting and killing what it means to be civilized'?"

John Rourke stared down at the battleground, at the dead there.

Natalia whispered, "He wanted an answer. I didn't have any."

John Rourke didn't have any either.

Chapter Thirty-one

Vladmir Karamatsov walked slowly across the snow, the whirring of rotor blades in the distance, helicopter gunships on guard against attack by forces of the Underground City or by the Germans.

Natalia's voice.

It had been her voice.

Her voice had routed his forces, disrupted the attack.

A jet streaked overhead, rising from the airfield at the staging area to which he had withdrawn, but the jet and the others which followed it now, not going to do battle, but reconnaissance.

There were many options open to him.

The Germans could not have a sufficiently large force.

The defenses of the Underground City would be severely depleted.

If he took the Underground City, he would not have sufficient forces, between casualties and defections— eighteen hundred defected, three hundred and ninety-one killed at last count, two hundred more at least injured—to both defend the city and attack the Germans and the Eden Project and the Hekla Community.

Vehicles were still coming in, carrying supplies, the

less seriously wounded.

"Natalia," he said under his breath, into the wind.

His right hand fingered the butt of his pistol beneath the heavy coat he wore against the cold. It had been Rourke again, perhaps one of the ones who had disrupted the gas attack.

The gas. There was enough of the gas, all of it bled into the smaller cannisters now, that if the proper delivery system could be found—the gas.

He could turn his adversaries against each other, against themselves.

Vladmir Karamatsov closed his eyes, tight, very tight, so tightly that his eyes began to hurt him. He tried to make the picture he wanted come to life in his mind. And he could see it starting to form—John Rourke, eyes wide in madness, the body of Rourke's wife, the body of Rourke's daughter, the body of Rourke's Jew friend—He could see it, their bodies riddled with bullet wounds, limbs hacked away, a pistol in Rourke's one hand, a bloody knife in the other, Rourke's hands covered with their blood.

Michael Rourke—the one who looked so like his father. Michael Rourke, the madness gripping him. Locked in combat, father against son, their fists hammering against each other, John Rourke's hands finding his knife, the knife gouging into his son's face and neck and chest. The body still and dead beneath John Rourke.

Natalia screaming from the corner of the room. Rourke turning to her, his pistol empty, throwing down his knife.

Natalia's pistols—but they fall from her hands because she is crying, proclaiming her love for him—that she cannot kill him.

Rourke's hands closing around her neck, the whiteness of Natalia's skin reddening, purpling, her tongue swelling as it distended, drool mixed with blood oozing from between her lips.

A choked scream.

Vladmir Karamatsov opened his eyes.

He stared skyward. Sometimes, he wished there were a God. He whispered to the heavens now. "My hour will come. Inevitably. You can't stop me—even if you exist. And he can't stop me." He screamed at the sky now. "John Rourke cannot stop me! He cannot stop me! John Rourke cannot stop me!" and Vladmir Karamatsov, the Hero Marshal, began to laugh.

ASHES
by William W. Johnstone

OUT OF THE ASHES   (1137, $3.50)

Ben Raines hadn't looked forward to the War, but he knew it was coming. After the balloons went up, Ben was one of the survivors, fighting his way across the country, searching for his family, and leading a band of new pioneers attempting to bring American OUT OF THE ASHES.

FIRE IN THE ASHES   (1310, $3.50)

It's 1999 and the world as we know it no longer exists. Ben Raines, leader of the Resistance, must regroup his rebels and prep them for bloody guerrilla war. But are they ready to face an even fiercer foe—the human mutants threatening to overpower the world!

ANARCHY IN THE ASHES   (1387, $3.50)

Out of the smoldering nuclear wreckage of World War III, Ben Raines has emerged as the strong leader the Resistance needs. When Sam Hartline, the mercenary, joins forces with an invading army of Russians, Ben and his people raise a bloody banner of defiance to defend earth's last bastion of freedom.

BLOOD IN THE ASHES   (1537, $3.50)

As Raines and his rugged band of followers search for land that has escaped radiation, the insidious group known as The Ninth Order rises up to destroy them. In a savage battle to the death, it is the fate of America itself that hangs in the balance!

ALONE IN THE ASHES   (1721, $3.50)

In this hellish new world there are human animals and Ben Raines—famed soldier and survival expert—soon becomes their hunted prey. He desperately tries to stay one step ahead of death, but no one can survive ALONE IN THE ASHES.

DOOMSDAY WARRIOR
by Ryder Stacy

After the nuclear devastation of World War III, America is no more than a brutalized colony of the Soviet master. But only until Ted Rockson, soldier of survival, leads a rebellion against the hated conquerers . . .

DOOMSDAY WARRIOR	(1356, $2.95)
#2: RED AMERICA	(1419, $2.50)
#5: AMERICA'S LAST DECLARATION	(1608, $2.50)
#6: AMERICAN REBELLION	(1659, $2.50)
#7: AMERICAN DEFIANCE	(1745, $2.50)
#8: AMERICAN GLORY	(1812, $2.50)
#9: AMERICA'S ZERO HOUR	(1929, $2.50)